DUCKSCARES

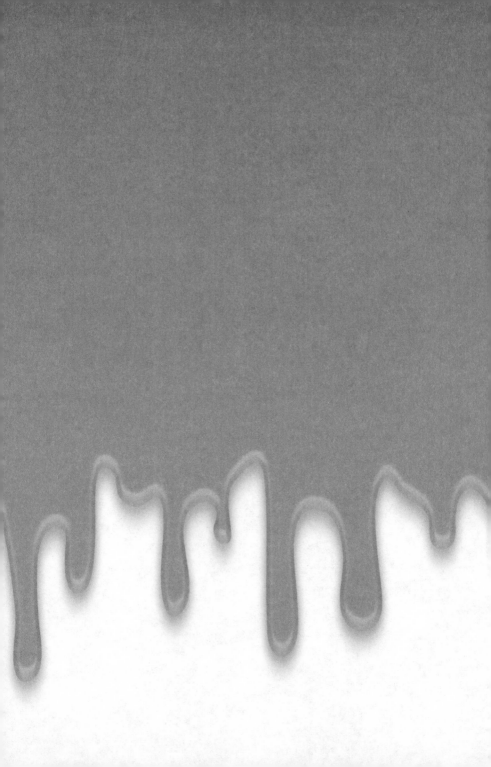

DISNEY
SPOOKYZONE

DUCKSCARES
THE NIGHTMARE FORMULA

BY TOMMY GREENWALD
ILLUSTRATED BY ELISA FERRARI

AMULET BOOKS • NEW YORK

Library of Congress Control Number 2020949640
ISBN 978-1-4197-5077-9

© 2021 Disney
Book design by Brenda E. Angelilli and Cheung Tai

Printed and bound in U.S.A.
10 9 8 7 6 5 4 3 2 1

Amulet Books are available at special discounts when purchased
in quantity for premiums and promotions as well as fundraising or
educational use. Special editions can also be created to specification.
For details, contact specialsales@abramsbooks.com or the address below.

Amulet Books® is a registered trademark of Harry N. Abrams, Inc.

ABRAMS The Art of Books
195 Broadway, New York, NY 10007
abramsbooks.com

PROLOGUE

The laboratory crackled and hissed as the light bulbs *BURNED* out one by one.

Soon it would be completely dark except for the sparks shooting out from the torn wires.

I could hear the **MAD SCIENTIST** cackling over his loudspeaker. He bellowed in his *EVIL* voice.

DON'T EVEN BOTHER TRYING TO RUN.

YOU CAN'T

ESCAPE!

As I ran through the **SLIMY** halls, I glanced behind me to make sure my brothers were still there. **"HUEY!"** I screamed. **"LOUIE! WHERE ARE YOU GUYS?"** I heard Huey's voice, but it sounded far away. **"WE'RE HERE! WE'RE COMING!"**

I turned around again, but all I saw was a giant green **MONSTER** with three yellowish-purple eyes blinking wildly.

HE WAS GAINING ON ME!

No, actually, he was gaining on ME.

You're both wrong. He was gaining on **ME.**

GUYS, YOU'RE RUINING THE TENSION!
LET'S JUST SAY HE WAS GAINING ON ALL THREE OF US.

fine.

OKAY.

So there we were, far from home, in the **SECRET LAB** of an evil genius, being chased by a monster, with no way out.

While I was trying to somehow **ESCAPE** with my life, one thing kept running through my head.

Hello, my name is **DEWEY DUCK**, and welcome to my story. It's called

DEWEY DUCK AND
THE **SPOOKY** SOCCER BALL.

Wait a second, hold up...that's not right.
We're going to need a new title.

A totally new title.

It's our story too. We're brothers.
We're a <u>TEAM.</u>

TEAM
~~DEWEY~~ SPOOKY
DUCK AND THE SOCCER
BALL

I get it. We're brothers. But everybody always says our names in the same order—Huey, Dewey, Louie—and it's not fair. I'm always in the **MIDDLE**.

Well, i'm always last.

Listen, you guys. Last is **COOL**. Last is **IMPORTANT**.

Like, you know that expression "save the best for last"? Like that. And first, well, obviously first is **FIRST**. It's where you want to be.

But the middle?

No one wants to be in the middle.

YOU GET MY POINT.

Yeah, I get your point, and you can narrate if you want, but we're not going to call the book DEWEY DUCK AND THE SPOOKY SOCCER BALL.

That's just not going to happen. And also, if you narrate, we get to chime in.

FINE.

Whenever we want.

FINE. JUST DON'T OVERDO IT.

We won't. Go ahead.

GREAT. So anyway, it all started when we went down one morning to eat.

MORNING, BOYS!

We were eating breakfast and Uncle Donald's phone **RANG**.

He picked it up and his face broke into a giant smile. **"YES!"** he exclaimed. **"OH, THAT'S AMAZING!"** And then he said things like **"WONDERFUL!"** and **"OH MY GOODNESS!"** and **"WOW!"** and **"I CAN'T WAIT TO TELL THEM."**

And then he hung up the phone and went back to eating breakfast.

We **STARED** at him. And stared some more. And some more.

But he just kept **EATING**.

After what felt like an eternity, all Uncle Donald told us was "That was the school calling. They would like us to meet in the principal's office before classes."

Huey, Louie, and I stopped **EATING**.
We stopped **MOVING**.
We might have even stopped **BREATHING**.

I **hate** the Principal's office.

I **hate** the Principal's office.

FINALLY, SOMETHING WE CAN ALL AGREE ON!

So we piled into the car, drove to school, and went into the principal's office, and even though Uncle Donald was smiling and whistling and acting happy, my brothers and I didn't **TRUST** it.

Nothing good ever happens in the principal's office.

NOTHING.

NUH—THING.

Oh, before I forget: do you want to know something funny about our school? It's called **HILLSIDE SCHOOL**, but it's not on a hillside at all; in fact, it's right near the ocean.

HILLSIDE SCHOOL
· DUCKBURG, CALISOTA ·
No hills, no sides, just great kids!

But you know what? We didn't care. Me and my brothers **LOVED** school. Mostly, anyway.

So we were a little nervous when Uncle Donald led us inside. The principal, Dr. Fragler, was sitting behind her desk. Next to her was a man I didn't **RECOGNIZE**.

NEITHER DID I.

NEITHER DID I.

AH! THE TRIPLETS!

(People called us the triplets a lot.) "Now for the hard part: figuring out **WHO IS WHO!** Wait, don't tell me . . ." We did that thing we always do when people try to guess who we are, which is to just sit there and look as **IDENTICAL** as possible.

It's more fun. But the truth is we're very **DIFFERENT**—as different as three brothers can be!

Well, yeah, of course we **LOOK** alike. We're triplets, remember? Here's the best way to tell us apart physically: Huey wears **RED**; I wear **BLUE**; and Louie wears **GREEN**.

BUT we also act very differently. So actually, the best way to remember who's who is by our personalities.

Huey is **HEROIC**; he is the bravest of all the brothers. He's also handy, another "H" word. He can fix anything. Bicycles, computers–you name it, he can fix it.

The only thing he can't fix is his looks.

Hey! That's not funny.
And besides, you look just like me.

Hmmm, he makes a good point.

Where was I? Oh yeah. I, Dewey, am *DASHING*. Meaning I'm extremely handsome. You get it, right?

And Louie? Well, he's not going to want to hear this, but Louie is **LEERY**. He's very cautious. Nervous.

Louie! Are you going to take that? HE's calling you a fraidy-cat!

Huey, stop yelling! You scared me!

OH BOY. THAT'S BAD TIMING.

We also each have one thing we're **MOST** afraid of. Huey is most afraid of **SNAKES**. (I can't think of anything else he's afraid of.) I'm most afraid of **BEES** (and heights, but mostly bees). Louie is most afraid of **EARTHQUAKES** (and many other things, even though he won't admit it).

So that's the best way to tell us apart, but I wasn't sure it was worth telling Dr. Flagler all that. She would just forget and ask us who was who the next time she saw us anyway.

"I'm **HUEY**," Huey said.

"I'm **DEWEY**," I said.

"I'm **LOUIE**," Louie said.

"Wonderful!" said Dr. Flagler. "Please, all of you, have a seat." She was being so nice! Usually, when you're in the principal's office, the principal acts less nice.

I glanced at my brothers.
Maybe we weren't in **TROUBLE** after all!

The guy we didn't know gave us a bright smile, and Dr. Flagler cleared her throat. "**THIS IS MR. RICHARD RICHARDS**," she told us.

"He is here from the **NATIONAL ASSOCIATION OF STUDIOUS AND TALENTED YOUTH**."

Uncle Donald giggled just a little bit.
"Otherwise known as **NASTY?**" he asked.

The man named Richard Richards stopped smiling for just a second. "We prefer not to call it that," he said. "Unfortunately, we didn't realize the acronym until after we made the name official."

"Be that as it may," Dr. Flagler said, "Mr. Richards is here to give you boys some **EXCITING** news."

"Yes, indeed." Mr. Richard Richards assumed a very official stance. "Every year we study students all across the world and evaluate them in terms of scholarship, attitude, and kindness to become **INTERNATIONAL STUDENT AMBASSADORS**. These students will travel to foreign **COUNTRIES**, where they will live with a hometown family while participating in the **EXCHANGE** program."

Right then, Louie kicked me in the leg for no reason.

I did not!

YES, YOU DID.

Oh, right, I did. That's because you weren't paying attention. You were staring out the window, thinking about who knows what!

THAT'S PROBABLY TRUE.

Anyway, where was I? Oh yeah—the man from **NASTY**. Right then, he paused, and we all leaned forward in suspense.

"It is my great pleasure to announce that Huey Duck, Dewey Duck, and Louie Duck have been **SELECTED** to be the International Student Ambassadors."

WAIT,
WHAT?!?!?!

I glanced at my brothers. I just wanted to make sure they were as excited and confused as I was, and I could tell just by looking at them that they were.

Huey, Louie, and I then did what any three brothers would do after hearing such news.

WE HOLLERED. LOUDLY. It sounded something like this:

YOWSAAAARAMA!

I think it sounded more like
"wEUTUEHRHHHHAAOOAHH!"

Actually, you're both wrong. It was this exactly:
"MaMABWBTRALLLLEEEIFIRIRIRIIRI!!!!!"

Can we at least all agree that we were excited?

As we whooped and hollered, Uncle Donald hugged us three tightly. "I confess, I did know a little something about this news ahead of time, but I wanted it to be a **SURPRISE**," he told us.

"Are you surprised?"

"YES!!!!" we answered.

We had about a **MILLION** questions, of course, but we each settled for one.

"what country are we going to first?"

"WHERE WILL WE LIVE?"

"HOw long will we be there?" was mine.

"There will be plenty of time to tell you everything," said Mr. Richards, "but for now, I will answer your first three questions. You will be going to the town of Berlin in **GERMANY**; you will live with a family, who has a niece who goes to the same school you will go to, for two months before moving on to your next destination."

"This is an incredible honor," Principal Flagler said. "But you children must remember that while you have been chosen for your playful and friendly personalities, you must promise to behave appropriately and not get into any trouble along the way."

"I couldn't agree more," added Uncle Donald, looking proudly at us. Can I get serious for a second, you guys?

SURE.

YEAH, GO AHEAD.

Great, thanks.

Because right at that moment, we looked at each other and we realized that our lives had just changed **FOREVER**. We were about to go on the **ADVENTURE OF A LIFETIME**—and the best part was we could do it together! But before we could start our adventure, I had one last question I wanted to ask, and it was very, very important. "Do they have **CHOCOLATE** in Germany?"

"Oh yes," said Mr. Richards. "They have some of the best chocolate in the world."

This time, we **CHEERED** so loud I think the entire town of Duckburg heard it.

CHAPTER
3

So, first things first: *THE PLANE RIDE*.

Uncle Donald drove us to the airport, and the car ride was pretty quiet. I guess we were a little nervous.

He kept saying, "This is going to be the **GREATEST** adventure of your lives," and we knew he was right—but still, the idea of being away from home for that long was pretty scary, to be honest. But then… **THEN** … we saw the airport, and the planes taking off and landing, and it was the **COOLEST** thing we'd ever seen. And heard. Because man, planes are **LOUD!**

We went to the gate, where we hugged Uncle Donald goodbye.

"Stay in touch!" he said. "I'm going to visit, but until I do, I want you to write to me, text me, video call me *EVERY OTHER DAY* at least!"

"We will, we promise!" we said, and we all kept hugging for a long time. I'm pretty sure Uncle Donald was wiping his eyes as he walked away. It's possible I was, too.

But I wasn't. Nope. Not me.
        I wasn't, either. I don't cry.

You were both crying, and you know it.

fine, but you have
        to tell everybody?!?!?!?

Our tears dried pretty fast, though—as soon as we boarded the plane. Can I tell you guys a secret?

I LOVE BEING ON A PLANE!

No you don't! You get bored after *FIVE* seconds!

THREE SECONDS, NOT EVEN *FIVE!*

Don't pay any attention to them. All you need to know is that Louie and Huey were just as excited as I was getting on that plane.

We were just settling into our seats and chattering excitedly when a tall man and a tall woman came over to us. They were wearing **SUPER COOL**, very official uniforms.

"I understand we have some **HONORED GUESTS** with us today," said the tall woman.

"I'm Captain Messing, and this is Captain Lardner, and we're delighted to be able to fly you over to Germany tonight." We all looked at each other and had the same exact reaction:

YAY!

The takeoff was loud, and fast, and exciting, and then dinner came, and it was delicious (whoever said airplane food is bad was **WRONG**), and then it started to get dark out, and then I got really, really tired. And so did my brothers.

And then, I guess, I fell asleep.

So did i.

So did I.

We all dreamed about what Germany was like.

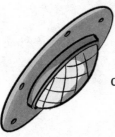

Then, the next thing we knew, a voice came over the plane's speakers.

"PLEASE PUT UP YOUR TRAY TABLES, PUT ON YOUR SEAT BELTS, AND RETURN TO YOUR SEATS TO THEIR FULL UPRIGHT POSITION. WE ARE IN OUR FINAL DESCENT IN OUR APPROACH TO THE BERLIN AIRPORT."

Well, that woke us up. We'd arrived! **GERMANY!** Huey rubbed his eyes, Louie stretched his legs, and I yawned for about twenty-eight seconds.

We all looked out the window in wonder as the wheels touched down.

FIRST THINGS FIRST: WE NEED TO FIND SOME CHOCOLATE!

Huey said.

CHAPTER 4

As soon as we got off the plane, we spotted a man holding up a sign that said:

INTERNATIONAL STUDENT AMBASSADORS PROGRAM.

"**Look, you guys!**" said Huey. "**THAT'S US!**" The man smiled, waved, and hurried over.

"**WELCOME TO GERMANY!**" he said as we all shook hands. "My name is Helmut Scholl. Let's go gather up your luggage."

"One thing you should know about us is I wear **RED**; Dewey wear **BLUE**; and Louie wears **GREEN**. So my suitcase is the red one," Huey said.

"And Dewey's is blue, and Louie's is green."

"We wear the same colors every day," I added.

"That's one of the ways people tell us apart," Louie double-added. Mr. Scholl smiled.

"Well, that's helpful to know. We're off, then!"

In the car, Mr. Scholl told us about the people we would be staying with. They were named **THE KELLERS**. Herr Keller, the uncle, and Frau Keller, the aunt, ran a small grocery store in the center of Berlin. They also had a niece, Sophie, who lived with them and was a fifth grader at the local school.

"They sound awesome," Huey said. As we drove to the Kellers' house, we looked out the window and took in the **FIRST** foreign country we'd ever been in.

"Hey, you guys, you know what?" Louie whispered.

"Germany looks kind of like Home!"

He was right. **"Where are the castles?"** Huey asked Mr. Scholl. "In my dream, there were a lot of castles."

Mr. Scholl laughed. "Oh, we absolutely have castles. They're just more in the countryside. One day soon, I will take you to see one."

Huey sat back with a satisfied grin. "I bet it'll be **HUGE!**" After about twenty more minutes, we pulled into the driveway of a small house with a small front yard. There was a young girl reading in a chair on the porch.

Ladies and gentlemen, Sophie Keller!!

You had such a crush on her, Huey.

I did not.

Let's let the readers decide, shall we?

ugh.

"Is she reading a comic book?" said Louie.

I LOVE COMIC BOOKS!

Huey, meanwhile, hadn't taken his eyes off the girl.

"Who is that?" he asked.

"Why, that's Sophie," said Mr. Scholl. "I told you about her, remember?"

Huey refused to blink, in case that would make him miss something she did. "Oh, yeah."

Dewey, you're being ridiculous! Stop exaggerating.

He's not exaggerating. You didn't blink for like five minutes.

We jumped out of the car, and the girl on the porch looked up from her book.

HELLO! we said, almost at the exact same time, although I think Huey might have been a little ahead of us. She waved back shyly.

I took a step forward.

"We're from America, and we're here to get to know your local customs and community, because it's very important that we all get to know and understand each other all over the world."

Hold up. You didn't say that at all.

In fact, you didn't say anything, because you're shy around girls.

He's right, Dewey. You didn't say that.

HUEY DID.

Okay, fine. So now you guys care about the details all of a sudden?

Huey took a step forward. "We're from America, and we're here to get to know your local customs and community, because it's very important that we all get to know and understand each other all over the world."

"That's right, we sure are," said Louie.

I was very shy around girls, so I just nodded.

TRUTH.
TRUTH.

The girl set down her book, came down off the porch, and walked up to us. I can't be totally sure, but I think she smelled like daffodils.

"My name is **SOPHIE**," she said. "Welcome to Germany." Huey, Louie, and I all blurted out one of the ten German words we'd learned to that point.

"**DANKE**," we said.

That's not true, Dewey. You and I said, "Danke," but Huey said,

"Frheghehkigigigig,"

because he was too nervous to form any actual words.

That's not true and you know it!

It is too true!

LOOK—THERE'S THE PICTURE TO PROVE IT!

FRHEGHEHKIGIGIGIG.

CHAPTER 5

Sophie's aunt and uncle turned out to be very **nice,** and they fed us an incredible meal of soup, potatoes, and an amazingly delicious apple strudel.

"I think I'm going to like it here," Louie said, but you could barely understand him, because his mouth was full.

The next day, it was time for school.

"You will like our school," Sophie told us. "It is very much fun, and you will learn a lot."

The walk to school was about ten minutes. It cut through the heart of the town, which was filled with bakeries, donut shops, butcher shops, and all the delicious smells you can imagine.

"I know we just had breakfast," Louie said, "but I'm starving."

"You're **ALWAYS** starving," I reminded him.

We turned a corner, and there stood the most interesting building in the whole town.

The outside walls sagged a bit and looked a little run-down, but the window panes were beautifully painted, the door was bright red, and a **GIANT SLANTED ROOF** sat above it all.

It almost looked like a gingerbread house come to life.

I LOVE gingerbread.

That's not important right now. Let Dewey tell his story.

So it's okay when you interrupt but not okay when I interrupt?

Yes.

We stared up at the building in wonder. Above the red door were two large signs with gold lettering. One said something in German that we didn't understand. But the other one was in English, and that one we did understand:

"Wow," Huey said.

"I love sports."

"and I love toys," Louie said.

"AND I LOVE EMPORIUMS,"

I said for some reason.

They all looked at me.

"You do?" asked Huey.

"Well, I don't know what they are exactly, but if I did, I would definitely love them!" I said. Sophie giggled.

"Can we go in the store?" Huey asked.

"Just for a minute?" But Sophie shook her head. "It's not open yet."

Louie pointed. "Hey, there in the window. That **MUST BE DR. Z!** Maybe we can get him to open the store?"

We all looked at the building, and sure enough, there was an older man looking at us through the window. He smiled and waved.

"Not now, Louie," Sophie said. "You don't want to be **LATE** for school on your first day!"

As we walked away, I glanced back to see if old Dr. Z was still in the window, but he was **GONE**.

"Can we go back after school?" Huey asked Sophie.

"We shall see," she said.

Two minutes later we walked into the schoolyard, and the first thing we saw was a giant sign:

WELCOME OUR
AMERICAN STUDENT
AMBASSADORS:
HUEY, DEWEY, AND
LOUIE DUCK!

And underneath the words, there was a drawing of the three of us, and it was pretty good, too!

Wait a second, hold on, that's not the actual picture at ALL.

Yeah, Dewey, is this a joke?

OKAY, OKAY, FINE.

Yep, that's the actual picture.

THE WHOLE SCHOOL WAS THERE TO GREET US!

We made our way to our first class of the day, which was already filled with lots of students.

Sophie saw me looking at one such napping boy.

"That's **HANS**," she said, tapping the boy on the head. Hans woke up.

"Nice to meet you," he said with a lazy smile. "Maybe you can come to my soccer match." Then he fell back asleep.

Sophie shrugged. "He needs his rest, because he has a very important game tomorrow," she said. "He's a wonderful soccer player, but not such a wonderful student."

• • •

Finally, it was time for **LUNCH!** Huey, Louie, and I couldn't wait. If it was anything like dinner the night before, we were in for a treat! Except it wasn't **ANYTHING** like dinner the night before.

UGH.
Don't make me think about it.
THEN DON'T.

I'M trying not to, but he's telling the story!
I'LL BE QUICK.

Lunch turned out to be all about **CABBAGE**.

Have you ever had cabbage?

It's hard to describe. It's kind of like salad, but cooked. It's **PURPLE**.

DELICIOUS

THE OPPOSITE OF DELICIOUS

Clearly, we were not thrilled. But you know who seemed to like it?

SOPHIE.

She was eating cabbage after cabbage. So was Hans, her nap-taking, soccer-playing friend. And so were two other kids.

Huey, Louie, and I stared at them, amazed.

Sophie glanced up at the three of us. "Oh, I forgot to tell you!" she said, her cheeks bulging. "We have a **CABBAGE–EATING CONTEST** every Monday. Do you guys want to join in?"

Huey, Louie, and I looked at each other in sheer **TERROR**.

"What do we do?" Huey asked.

"Well," Louie said.

"It would be rude not to take part in their tradition!" Then they both looked at me.

A hot flash of **PANIC** ran through my body. "What?" I said. "What are you guys looking at me for?"

"You've always been the most adventurous eater of the three of us," Louie said, and he was right.

One time, when we were younger, Dewey actually ate a chocolate-covered worm for a nickel.

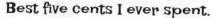

Best five cents I ever spent.

SO THAT WAS HOW I JOINED THE SCHOOL'S CABBAGE-EATING CONTEST.

And guess what. Cabbage isn't as bad as you think once you start shoveling it into your mouth as fast as you can. It's **WORSE**.

I can still remember the expression on your face.

Like a horror movie, but worse.

The winner was Hans, so it turned out he was good at playing soccer, napping, *AND* eating cabbages.

I went up to Hans and shook his hand. "Well done," I said.

"Thanks," he said, and then he **BURPED**.

I looked down and noticed he had a soccer ball at his feet. "Sophie said you were a **TERRIFIC** soccer player."

"I'm never without a ball," he told me. "I eat with it, I sleep with it, I walk around with it all day, except for when my teachers make me put it away."

He picked up the ball and hugged it.

"It's *MY BEST FRIEND*."

"I feel the same way about french fries," I told him.

My brothers ran up to me and started slapping me on the back. "That was *AMAZING!*" Louie said. "Your brother did very well," Hans told them. "Especially for a newcomer."

Sophie joined us. "The boys are going to come to your game tomorrow, Hans."

"Will you be there?" Hans asked her.

She grinned. "Of course!"

He grinned back.

That was the moment I realized that maybe Hans and Sophie liked each other.

Ugh. Do you have to tell this part?

Of course he does.
It's an important part of the plot.

No it isn't!

Your concern has been duly noted.
Dewey, keep going.
You're just about to get to the good stuff.

Ah, yes, the good stuff.
You know what the only thing better than the good stuff is?

what?

The scary stuff.

WELL, YOU CAN BOTH RELAX . . .
BECAUSE IT'S ALL COMING UP.

CHAPTER

6

After school, Sophie gave in to our constant begging and agreed to take us to **DR. Z'S TOY AND SPORTS EMPORIUM**.

Hans came with us, because it was on his way home, too. The inside of the store was just as cool as the outside. There were tons of little rooms, each painted a different color, with all kinds of toys: old toys, new toys, big toys, small toys, simple toys, and complicated toys.

There were parents and children everywhere, running around, trying out the toys and laughing. The only thing that seemed to be missing was the **OWNER** himself.

We were in the yellow
room when I asked Sophie:

We all turned around to see a
rather elderly man standing there,
wearing a white lab coat over a
very nice suit.

"Wow!" said
Louie. "You just
appeared out of
nowhere."

"Just another one of my tricks,
I suppose." The man bowed.

DR. Z, AT YOUR SERVICE.

"This is the coolest store I've
ever been in!" exclaimed Huey.
"Where did you get all these **TOYS?**"

"Toys have always been my passion," said Dr. Z.
"My greatest pleasure in life is to bring joy to young
people with toys and games."

He peered at my brothers and me.

"Are you fellows new around here? I don't believe I've seen you before."

"This is **HUEY**, **DEWEY**, and **LOUIE**," Sophie said.

"They're the new students from America, and they're staying with me."

"Well, welcome to our little town," said Dr. Z. "I hope you find it very much to your liking."

"We love it so far," I said. "Everyone has been so nice." Dr. Z. smiled.

"That's **WONDERFUL**."

His hands, which had been behind his back the whole time, suddenly emerged, and he was holding **A SMALL BOX**.

"The occasion of your arrival would seem to merit the offering of a **GIFT**," he said. "May I present this as a small offering of welcome."

We looked at each other, and then Louie walked up and accepted the box.

We opened the box and pulled out this very **AWESOME KALEIDOSCOPE**.

"Hans, me, and the rest of the kids in the neighborhood got one from Dr. Z when the store first opened. They're super cool," said Sophie.

She was right: it was **SUPER COOL**.

We took turns looking into it, but none of us saw the same thing. I saw colors, and Huey saw stars at night, and Louie saw rippling waves on the ocean.

When I looked through the kaleidoscope, it felt like I was in a **DAZE**, and it seemed like something happened that I didn't remember.

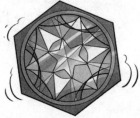

But I decided it was just because I was tired from all the excitement of landing in a new country.

ME TOO.

ME THREE.

Dr. Z smiled, then glanced at Hans.

"You're the boy who scores all those goals on the soccer team. Am I correct?"

Hans smiled shyly. "I guess so."

"Well, I have a **SPECIAL PRESENT** for you, as well." And again seemingly out of nowhere, Dr. Z passed a soccer ball to Hans.

Hans juggled it on his feet a few times. Dr. Z bowed again. "Thank you for stopping by. I must bid you farewell." Then he walked away.

"Gosh, I love the way he talks," said Huey. "So **FANCY**."

Sophie looked at her watch. "We'd better go," she said. "I told my aunt and uncle I'd have you home by four."

Hans picked up his new soccer ball and looked at it carefully. It was purple with yellow designs, but when he twirled it in the light, it looked like it changed colors—almost like the kaleidoscope.

CHAPTER
7

The next day after school, we went to Hans's soccer game, and I couldn't believe how many people had shown up. All the kids from school were there, and so were the teachers!

Dr. Z was there, too, and he gave us a friendly wave.

"GOOD LUCK, YOUNG MAN!" he yelled to Hans, who was warming up with his teammates out on the field.

Hans waved back at Dr. Z. "Thanks, and thanks again for the **BALL!**"

The game started, and boy, was it exciting. Hans was **GREAT**. He raced up and down the field, controlling the ball at his feet as if with **MAGNETS**, making beautiful passes, shooting **AMAZING SHOTS**, and **STEALING** the ball away from the other team. But despite all his incredible skill, he couldn't score.

NO ONE COULD SCORE!

As the game wound down, it looked like it might end in a 0–0 tie. But then, with about **FOUR** minutes to go, Hans got the ball near his own goal line.

He sprinted up the field, dribbled past about three opponents, then passed it to one of his teammates. The teammate took one dribble, then kicked the ball toward the opponent's goal line.

It looked way too far away for anyone to catch up to it, but all of a sudden, Hans came **OUT OF NOWHERE**.

He beat everyone to the ball, turned quickly, and **FIRED** it toward the goal.

It was just out of the goalkeeper's reach.

It nestled in the netting and fell to the ground.

Everyone watching the game let out a **MIGHTY ROAR** and started jumping up and down on each other, which was exactly what the players on Hans's team were doing.

A few minutes later, the referee **BLEW** the whistle for the end of the game, and everyone jumped on everyone else all over again.

"WE WON!" Sophie yelled over and over.

WE WON WE WON WE WON!

Everyone poured onto the field to celebrate with the players.

Huey, Louie, and I hung back, but Sophie saw us and turned around.

"This means we made the **LEAGUE CHAMPIONSHIP!** Come celebrate with us! **YOU** guys are **PART OF THIS TOWN NOW!**"

A little while later, after the celebration simmered down, we waited for Hans to come out of the locker room. Even though it was right after the game, he had a **BALL** at his feet.

It was the cool yellow-and-purple one Dr. Z had given him.

"GREAT GAME!" we told him. "Thanks," he said, kicking the ball to himself.

Uh, excuse me, Dewey?
   Just FYI, the ball wasn't yellow and purple.
It was more like PURPLE AND YELLOW.

   Are you serious right now?
No one cares. And besides, don't distract Dewey,
he's just about to get to the cool part.

Oh yeah, true. My bad, Dewey, go ahead.

SO LIKE I WAS SAYING . . .

Hans had Dr. Z's yellow-and-purple ball at his feet, and he was doing this thing where he was kicking it to himself in the air, and it **NEVER TOUCHED THE GROUND**. Even while he was talking to us, he **NEVER** missed.

Finally, Huey said, "Hey, Hans, how do you do that?" Hans glanced up at Huey, then back at the ball.

"What, this? This is called juggling. It just takes a lot of practice."

"CAN YOU TEACH US?" Louie asked.

"Sure." As we circled up around him, Hans said, "The first thing you need to do is—" And then he **STOPPED TALKING**.

The ball fell to the ground. Then his eyes opened **REALLY WIDE** to the point where it looked like they might fall out. And then, believe it or not, he started running around in a circle and yelling:

TORNADO! TORNADO! TORNADO!

Everyone looked around in a **PANIC**. Tornado? Was there a tornado **COMING?**

The sky was totally blue, and it wasn't windy at all. **WHAT** was Hans talking about?

But he kept running around, looking scared out of his wits, his arms flailing wildly. **"IT'S COMING! A TORNADO IS COMING! THE WORST TORNADO OF ALL TIME! I HATE TORNADOES! RUN!!!!"**

Then, while he was running around like a wild person, he tripped and **FELL FACE-FIRST** into a puddle

that had formed the night before. And just like that, Hans stopped flailing and yelling.

Sophie went up to him. "Hans? Are you okay?" He was breathing hard, and his eyes were still a little wild-looking, but he nodded.

"Wha–what happened?" he asked.

"WHAT HAPPENED?" Sophie snorted out a nervous laugh. **"YOU WERE RUNNING AROUND LIKE A CRAZY PERSON, SCREAMING ABOUT TORNADOES!"**

Hans looked shocked. "Are you sure you didn't *IMAGINE* the whole thing?"

We all shook our heads. "We're sure," Sophie said.

"GOSH." Hans got to his feet but still seemed a little wobbly. "I've been *SCARED* of tornadoes my whole life. But still, that makes no sense. All of a sudden I was in the middle of *HUNDREDS* of tornadoes, all *SPINNING* toward me. Suddenly, I was falling, and then, just as quickly, I was wet on the ground, back with you guys."

Sophie shook her head. "Are you trying to *TRICK US?*"

My brothers and I walked over to Hans.

"Yeah, it's *NOT* funny!" I said.

"I'm totally fine! Do you want to continue our juggling lesson?"

"No, that's okay," Huey said. "You're tired from the game, and we should probably get going."

Hans picked up his soccer ball and took a deep breath, "That was the **STRANGEST** thing that's *EVER* happened to me."

Little did he know things were about to get *A WHOLE LOT STRANGER*.

CHAPTER

8

*T*he next day in school, we kept an eye on Hans to see if he was acting strange or unusual in any way, but he seemed totally normal.

He had his **SOCCER BALL** with him, as usual, and everyone was talking excitedly about the big championship game.

At recess, my brothers and I played around with our **NEW TOY** while hanging out with some of the other students.

Time flew while we were socializing with our new friends, and before we knew it, **FRAU SHULTZ**, one of the teachers, yelled, "Well, recess is nearly **OVER**. It's time for mathematics in **FIVE MINUTES!**" She walked away with a laugh as all the kids **HONKED** with displeasure at that **TERRIBLE** news.

Meanwhile, I decided to take one **LAST LOOK** into the kaleidoscope. As I twisted the kaleidoscope, the usual array of **GLORIOUS COLORS** and patterns **BURST** into view. When I lowered it from my face, the same dizziness as I'd had the first time I looked through it washed over me again.

"What?" said Huey, who was looking at me oddly.

"HUH?" I responded as I shook my head to clear it. "You whispered 'bees.' Is there one on my head?"

Louie looked around nervously, swatting at his hat.

"No I didn't."

"Oh, weird. Thought I heard you." Huey shrugged, then walked in with the rest of the kids, Louie behind him. Had I said something when I looked through the kaleidoscope?

I didn't remember, but I did feel a little STRANGE.

Anyway, the next day we were going to Hans' practice–

Hey sorry to interrupt. It's me, Louie.
I think Dewey is doing a great job so far,
don't you guys?
Let's hear it for Dewey!

Okay, enough of that.
I think it's time for
someone else to tell
the story for a little
while. So to recap:
We were given this amazing honor,
we went to Germany, we moved in with a
family, we met Sophie, we started going

to school, we met Hans, we went to a cool store and met Dr. Z, everyone was so nice to us, then we went to Hans's soccer game and he was the hero, but after the game he acted really weird but didn't even remember acting weird, then the next day in school Dewey was looking through the kaleidoscope when we thought we heard him mutter something about bees.

Dewey said he didn't, though, but he was kind of freaked out and thought something spooky was going on.

And then he turned to me and said, "LOUIE, HELP ME! YOU'RE DEFINITELY THE BRAVEST AND MOST COURAGEOUS OF ALL THE BROTHERS, SO I NEED YOU."

And so, of course, I—

Okay, okay, that'll do.

That'll do? What do you mean, "that'll do"?

I mean Dewey never said any of that, especially the part about you being the bravest and most courageous, so I'm going to have to ask you to give the story back to Dewey.

Are you serious right now?

Very. Dewey, please continue.

THANK YOU, HUEY.
NOW I'M ABOUT TO TELL THE PART ABOUT HANS'S SOCCER PRACTICE.
IT'S IMPORTANT, BECAUSE THAT'S WHEN THINGS STARTED REALLY GOING DOWN.

Absolutely.

Yes, down down.

CHAPTER 9

As I was saying before I was so rudely interrupted, the next day we decided to go watch Hans' team practice. Sophie said it would be fun, and besides, we wanted to make sure Hans was okay being back on the field after his tornado episode.

As the players did their stretching, my brothers and I tried to do the same stretches.

It did not go well.

I could touch my toes, but Louie could only touch his knees.

That's true.

I could do twenty sit-ups, but Dewey could only do four.

THAT'S TRUE.

I could do thirty leg lifts, but Huey couldn't even do **one**.

That's **NOT** true!

Okay, you could do one.

That's true.

Then it was time to play **ACTUAL SOCCER**. And that was when things went haywire. As soon as someone—anyone—on Hans's team touched the ball, something **STRANGE** happened.

The first kid who kicked the ball started spinning around in circles and yelling, **"NO! NOT PIANO PRACTICE AGAIN!"**

The second kid who kicked the ball started hopping around and beelined it toward the bleachers while screaming, **"THE FLOOR IS LAVA!"**

The third kid who kicked the ball curled up on the ground, rocking back and forth and muttering, **"NOT GREAT-AUNT GERTRUDE'S FRUITCAKE."**

The fourth kid who touched the ball started running backward, bumping into people, and mumbling **MATH EQUATIONS** over and over again.

The fifth kid was Hans—and just like he had the day before, he started screaming about **TORNADOES COMING**. Huey, Louie, Sophie, and I stared at each other.

WHAT WAS HAPPENING?

We looked around for the coaches, but they were up busy by the fence, working on something. In any case, they were not paying attention to what was happening.

We ran out onto the field just as the goalkeeper picked up the ball. He immediately ran to the nearest goalpost, began to **CLIMB** it, and started hollering, "Please get that cat away from me! I don't like cats!"

"Oh boy," Sophie said.

WE NEED TO DO SOMETHING!

She looked around, then noticed a giant container of water on a bench. "Help me, you guys!" she said. We didn't question why, and we ran over as fast as we could, helped carry the container to all the players who were doing crazy things, and started **DOUSING THEM** with water. And **IT WORKED!**

It was like the water woke them up, and they all stopped immediately.

"WHOA," I said.

"That worked," Huey said. Sophie smiled proudly.

"I figured water could help us wake them up!"

"You're a genius," Huey told her with love in his eyes.

CUT IT OUT!

TEE HEE HEE!

Sorry.

Anyway, the kids had dazed and confused looks on their faces as they walked off the field.

Hans was **SHAKING** his head back and forth, like he knew something really weird had just happened but he wasn't sure exactly what it was.

After all the players exited the field, we looked at it suspiciously. Then Huey took a few steps forward, examining the grass.

"WHAT ARE YOU DOING?" I called to him.

"Doing some sleuthing and trying to figure out what in the world is happening here," Huey called back.

The rest of us followed, also scrutinizing the **GRASS**. "Maybe the field has magic powers or something?"

"Maybe we should head back to the parking lot," Louie said urgently. We ignored his nerves and continued to search the grass, goalposts, and benches, trying to find anything to explain what was happening but came up with nothing.

Super strange, Huey said as we joined up in the middle of the field. Absentmindedly, he began dribbling Hans's forgotten ball between his feet.

"Maybe the team just ate something **WEIRD?**"

As I continued to think of an explanation, I distractedly waved to Huey to pass the ball, and he did so without thinking. We got a little distracted and began really kicking the ball back and forth.

And then, just like that, we weren't there anymore.

This part is hairy.

I still can't believe I wasn't there.

You sound like you're jealous!

Of course I'm not jealous! It's just that . . . well, I kind of wish maybe I'd been there with you guys.

It was terrifying!

Yeah, terrifying in, like, a cool way right?

No! Terrifying in a terrifying way!

Yeah, I get that.

As soon as I touched that soccer ball, it felt like my mind and my body started **SPINNING IN A CIRCLE**. There was a sudden flash of light, the sky turned a **DARK PURPLE**, and suddenly I was **FLYING** above the ground, upside down, staring at the grass.

I shot up into the sky, and then started plummeting back toward the ground—**FASTER, FASTER, FASTER**—headfirst, like a cliff diver.

Except there was no water.

And then there was another flash of light, and I was standing in a forest, and the air was *FILLED WITH BEES*.

Remember *I AM MORE AFRAID OF BEES* than anything else in the world? I heard a voice:

"Dewey! Dewey!"

I saw my brother Huey standing on the other side of a path.

I started to cross it, but he yelled, **"DON'T"** and pointed down. There was a pit filled with *SNAKES* in his path.

That happened to be the thing Huey was more afraid of than anything else in the world.

Neither one of us knew what to do.

"HOW CAN I GET TO YOU?" I shouted at him.

"I'LL COME TO YOU!" Huey shouted back. He climbed up a tree and started wriggling across a long branch that stretched across the path, but his legs were shaking, and halfway across he lost his balance and started to fall.

"hELP! HELP, DEWEY!"

One of the biggest snakes—maybe **THE BIGGEST**— reached up and opened his massive jaws, as if waiting for Huey to fall. I realized there was no time to waste, so I started tiptoeing around the pit, swatting at the bees, trying to avoid the snakes.

I grabbed Huey's hand, he jumped down, and we managed to sprint back to my side of the path, with the **SNAPPING JAWS** of snakes following our every step. We looked at each other, trying to catch our breath.

"NOW WHERE DO WE GO? WHAT HAPPENED? HOW DID WE END UP HERE???" asked Huey.

I pointed at an opening in the woods. "THAT WAY!"

We started running, but when I looked behind us, I saw that the bees and snakes had **MORPHED** together into some sort of **HALF-SNAKE, HALF-BEE MONSTER**, slithering and flying, with flicking tongues that were lashing out just behind our ears.

We ran faster, and the snake monsters flew faster. I noticed the bright purple sky just up ahead, where the tree line ended, and I realized we weren't just running toward the edge of the woods—we were running toward the edge of the **WORLD**.

"IT'S A CLIFF!" Huey shouted.

"THERE'S NOWHERE TO GO!" I glanced behind us. The snake monsters were gaining on us. Their giant jaws were open, and their tongues were lashing out of their mouths, exposing endless rows of sharp teeth that looked ready to chew us up into a thousand tiny pieces.

THE CLIFF GOT CLOSER AND CLOSER. SO DID THE SNAKE MONSTERS. When we got to the edge, Huey and I hesitated. We had two choices, and neither one of them was very appealing. Meanwhile, the snake monsters were so **CLOSE** I could **SMELL** their breath.

It wasn't very pleasant.

"WE'RE JUST GOING TO HAVE TO JUMP AND HOPE FOR THE BEST!" Huey yelled.

"I'LL SEE YOU AT THE BOTTOM!" I yelled back. We closed our eyes and made the leap.

AAAAAAAHHHHHHHHHH!

we both said.

It seemed like we were in the air forever, tumbling head over feet as the wind howled in our faces.

I looked down but could see no ground. We kept screaming and screaming as we fell until . . .

SPLASH!

I opened my eyes, and the first thing I saw was my brother Louie holding an empty bucket. I could tell by his face that he was worried and confused.

I bet you were happy to see me, huh?

VERY.

And the next thing I saw was my other brother, Huey, who was right next to me. We were both soaking wet. "What happened?" I asked Louie.

"You were both doing **WEIRD STUFF** like the other kids! I had to throw a bucket of water on you to wake you up!"

Yeah! Thanks for that, brother! I almost drowned!

Come on! Don't be so dramatic!

We both looked around and realized we were right back on the soccer field. During our **DREAM** we must have fallen on the ground.

"Are you two all right?" asked Louie.

"I guess so," I answered. "I mean, considering we were in a *JUNGLE* full of *BEES* and *SNAKES*, and then the bees and snakes turned into *SNAKE MONSTERS*, and the only way we could escape them was by jumping off a cliff with *NO PARACHUTE* or anything."

Louie glanced at Sophie, who was right next to him. She looked at me and said, "Uh, Dewey? You've been standing here *THE WHOLE TIME*."

"Yeah," said Louie. "The only weird thing that happened is that you and Huey were *RUNNING* around in a circle for a few seconds, yelling, 'Jump!, Jump!, I hate bees!, I hate snakes!,' And then you fell."

"Just *NOW?*" Huey asked.

Hans nodded. "That's right. It was right after you and Dewey started playing with the *SOCCER BALL*."

"I told you there was *SOMETHING* about that ball," Louie said, sounding kind of like a know-it-all.

Well, what do you expect! I **DO** know it all!

Ha! You got lucky, like, that one time.

It's not luck, it's brilliance.

Ugh. Excuse me while
I get sick to my stomach.

All of a sudden, just like that, **IT CLICKED**.

EVERYONE knew what was going on.

Everyone turned to the **BALL**, which was just lying there, minding its own business, pretending to be perfectly **INNOCENT**. Then we looked at each other again and all realized something at the exact same time.

WE NEEDED TO PAY A VISIT TO KINDLY OLD DR. Z.

CHAPTER 10

The next day, **after school,** my brothers and I went over to Dr. Z's store.

It was crowded, as usual. But we weren't there to play games. We were there on a **MISSION**.

Oooh . . . I like the way that sounds.

Yeah, very cool. "A Mission." Let's do this.

When we walked in, I noticed a sign I hadn't seen earlier:

ALL TOYS and GAMES
DESIGNED and CREATED
by DR. Z!

"**WHOA,**" I said to myself. "**THIS GUY MUST BE SOME SORT OF GENIUS.**"

We hunted around for any sign of **MAGIC** soccer balls, or **WEIRD**, unusual balls of any kind, but everything we picked up seemed perfectly normal.

We tried to find **CLUES** to other possible **CREEPY TOYS** and tried to carefully watch Dr. Z without being noticed, but we had no luck.

Everything looked like a normal toy store and he was nowhere to be seen.

The only **STRANGE** thing we found was an old, dusty board game called **SETTLE THE SCORE** on display on a shelf on one side of the store.

Louie picked it up. "This is cool," he said. Then he started reading aloud from the box.

"Have you ever had someone do a bad thing to you and get away with it? That doesn't seem fair, right? Well, now all you have to do is open this box, and justice can be yours at last! Pick your enemy and plot your revenge in this thrilling, chilling game for all ages."

I was interrupted by a voice behind me.

"THAT'S ONE OF MY PROUDEST INVENTIONS."

We all turned around to see Dr. Z standing there. He reached out and took the box from my hands. "It's one of the first games that I invented. It was incredibly popular. Unfortunately, I'm completely out of stock and it's now out of production. That is the **ONLY COPY** I have left, and I'm afraid I have to leave it on display."

"Oh, sure thing," Huey said. "Uh . . . we were just looking at it. And, you know, it's cool, and, uh . . ."

Dr. Z smiled. "I very much appreciate your enthusiasm. If I find another one, I will gladly sell it to you! In the meantime, is there **ANYTHING ELSE** in the store I can interest you in?"

"What's **DOWN THERE?**" Louie asked. He was pointing at a stairway that looked like it went down to some sort of **BASEMENT**.

"Ah, that," said Dr. Z. "Why, that is my **LABORATORY**, where I dream up some of my most wonderful inventions."

Louie's eyes widened. "Can we see it?"

"I'm sorry, but it's not open to the public." He bowed, in that formal way he had. "I need to go check on the other clients now. Enjoy your visit, and please don't hesitate to find me if you see something else you like."

As we watched him walk away, Huey elbowed me in the ribs. "Did you hear him? We should **SNEAK IN** and try to go check out his lab!"

"Are you sure?" Louie asked. "I'm kind of getting a weird feeling from that guy. Also, what if he finds us? It could be **DANGEROUS!**"

"Yeah, I agree," I said.

Huey giggled. "You guys can't possibly be **SCARED** of a toy maker!"

"What about that ball of his?" Louie said.

"And who said anything about being scared?" I added defensively. "I just think we need a better plan. Plus, I'm hungry and I need a snack."

"Fine," Huey sighed. "But we should really find a way to **GET IN** there. I feel we would find all the answers to our questions and the **CLUES** we need to confirm he is connected to the mysterious **INCIDENTS**."

While we were discussing it, an announcement came over a loudspeaker in the store.

"HELLO, TOY AND GAME LOVERS, THIS IS YOUR OLD FRIEND DR. Z! THANK YOU ALL FOR COMING TODAY! WE WILL BE CLOSING IN TEN MINUTES. I HOPE TO SEE YOU ALL AGAIN VERY SOON!"

"You guys were a little scared," Huey said while we walked out. "Just admit it!"

ABSOLUTELY NOT!

But I was pretty glad to get out of that store. There was something that was giving me the chills.

CHAPTER 11

When we got home after the strange visit to Dr. Z's store, Frau Keller had a big smile on her face.

WE HAVE A SPECIAL INVITATION TONIGHT. WE'RE GOING TO THE CITY FAIR, AS SPECIAL GUESTS OF THE MAYOR!

WE LOVE FAIRS!

After driving for about fifteen minutes, we suddenly saw this giant open field ahead, with games, rides, food stands, and, on one side, a small white tent.

"Whoa," we all said. "What's that?"

"That's the Mystery Tent," said Herr Keller.

Huey elbowed me in the ribs.

"Cool! We should definitely check that one out!"

So it turns out that when it comes to fairs, you want to do as much as you can, but you don't want to *overdo* it. You need to pace yourself. For example, the first time I went on the Ferris wheel, it was great.

The second time, it was pretty good.

The third time, I felt **SICK**.

Meanwhile, Sophie rode the roller coaster five times and felt totally fine.

"Come on, you guys. Who wants to go with me again?" she asked.

I shook my head, still feeling **QUEASY**.

"Not me. I'm going to go sit down and listen to that nice band playing nice songs."

My brothers nodded in quick agreement. "Okay, fine," Sophie said, although she didn't seem happy about it.

But the band was great, and instead of sitting, we found ourselves dancing and singing along!

Hold up. Dewey and I danced. Huey stared at Sophie dancing.

THAT'S NOT TRUE. I DIDN'T DANCE TO THE FIRST SONG. I DANCED TO THE SECOND SONG.

When you slow danced with Sophie.

ALSO NOT TRUE.
AND STOP TALKING ABOUT SOPHIE ALL THE TIME. MAYBE YOU'RE THE ONE WHO HAS A CRUSH ON HER.

I'm ignoring you.

Dewey, please continue with your story.

AHA!

We danced for a while, until Sophie's aunt came and told us it was time for dinner. We headed to an area of the field where a bunch of picnic tables had been set up and people were going to sit. All around were other tables loaded with the greatest food you could ever imagine. And we were ready to try it all! There was also a podium with a microphone and, over it, a banner that read *WELCOME, HUEY, DEWEY, AND LOUIE!*

"Hey, that's us!" said Louie. "And that's where you're going to sit," Frau Keller told us, pointing at the table in the center. "There?" I said.

"Right at the center, where everyone can see us?"

She laughed. "Of course! You're the guests of honor. And no worries, Sophie will be with you."

"Why is he up there on the stage?" Louie asked.

"I guess that's why." Sophie pointed at another **SIGN** I hadn't noticed before.

CONGRATULATIONS TO
Dr. DEITRICH ZINZENFEFFER
CITIZEN OF THE YEAR!

Louie snorted. "**ZINZENFEFFER?** No wonder he goes by Dr. Z!"

Sophie's uncle, who was listening to our conversation, leaned over. "Professor Zinzenfeffer is a local. He was born in Berlin and spent his childhood here. Then, years ago, he moved away and became a very **FAMOUS** scientist and inventor. Recently he moved back to town, and he's been gracious enough to share with us his latest invention: a type of grass that is soft, lush, and never has to be cut. He already resurfaced one of our town soccer fields, as a gift!" Herr Keller pointed at the sign. "As you can see, the town is very grateful."

We all nodded, but I was thinking: *If it's anything like those soccer balls of his, we're in trouble.*

I was thinking the same exact thing.

So was I.

AND SO WAS I.

SOPHIE! What are you doing here?

WHY SHOULD I LET YOU BOYS HAVE ALL THE FUN? IT'S MY STORY, TOO, YOU KNOW. KIND OF.

Well, yeah, that's true, but your name isn't on the cover of the book.

IS IT TOO LATE TO ADD IT?

UHH . . .

SEE WHAT YOU CAN DO, OKAY? ANYWAY, WE WERE ALL THINKING THE SAME THING. IT WAS LOOKING MORE AND

MORE LIKE DR. Z WAS IN THE MIDDLE OF ALL THE STRANGE STUFF THAT WAS HAPPENING.

She's absolutely right. But I have to say, it's getting kind of crowded in here.

IN WHERE?

In this book.

OH. OKAY, WELL, I'LL LEAVE YOU GUYS TO IT.

I wanted to ask the others what they were thinking about Dr. Z. Just then he came over and smiled.

WELL, HELLO.

"How wonderful to see you again."

"Dr. Z," Sophie said, whispering so her aunt and uncle couldn't hear her. "My friend Hans kicked your soccer ball, and some very **STRANGE** things happened to him. And then, at the next practice, his whole team kicked the same ball and strange and scary things happened to them. And then my friends Huey and Dewey kicked the ball, and strange and scary things happened to them, too. Do you have anything to say?"

Dr. Z frowned. "Oh, my. It sounds like it's been a strange and scary time. But of course you're not saying it had anything to do with me or my present?"

I stepped in. "Well, what else could it be?" But before Dr. Z could answer, he was pulled away by another adult.

At first, everything was great: the appetizer, the main course, the entertainment between courses. (There was a string quartet playing music by someone named Beethoven.) And at one point

Huey was so full he even fell asleep. Once the main course ended, the mayor got up to make a speech.

"Welcome, citizens of Berlin! Tonight, we are here to welcome our young guests from *AMERICA*, Huey, Dewey, and Louie Duck, who will call Berlin home for the next two months; and also to honor one of our favorite friends, professor **DEITRICH ZINZENFEFFER**, who has recently returned to our town and generously given his time, resources, and brilliance to a fabulous new athletic field."

The mayor ges-
tured for us to stand
up, so we did, and
everyone started to
APPLAUD.

We waved, and
then Dr. Z stood up,
and he waved, too, and we all shook his hand again, took selfies, shook the mayor's hand, and then sat back down.

And after all the shaking of all the hands, dessert was served. It was well worth the wait! I can't really describe it except as this amazing gooey, chocolatey pastry thingie.

Which is not the technical term for it. And may I just say . . . YUM.

I echo that YUM and would like to add a DELISH!

AND I AM GOING TO COMBINE YOUR TWO WORDS, BECAUSE THE ONLY WAY TO DESCRIBE THAT MEAL WOULD BE YUMALICIOUS.

After two helpings of the gooey pastry thingie, we sat back in our chairs, stuffed. "I think we can all agree dinner was excellent," Huey said. "Now let's go back outside to the games and stuff."

Just then, the mayor walked over to our table. "Have you been to the Mystery Tent yet?" she asked.

We looked at each other.

"Not yet," I said.

"Oh, you must go!" said the mayor. "It takes you on a virtual adventure. Everyone is commenting on how they are having the most exciting time! Even I tried it."

"What was your adventure?" Huey asked.

The mayor clapped her hands together. "I went back to **DINOSAUR** times. It was wonderful! A little scary sometimes, as it looked so real!"

"Let's go, you guys," Sophie said, so we grabbed Hans and followed her to the tent.

The courtyard was **CROWDED** with fairgoers.

There were so many things to see and do.

We arrived at the white tent, which sat bathed in purple light. A sign above it read:

MYSTERY TENT:
TAKE THE ADVENTURE OF A LIFETIME!

On one side there was a booth with what we thought was a person—

Hey, let me tell this part.

YOU REALLY WANT TO, LOUIE?

Yup. I mean, I'm the one it happened to, right?

Right, but . . . are you sure you can handle it?

Of COURSE I can handle it.

You guys are so annoying!

OKAY, GO FOR IT.

So we go into the tent, and we suddenly hear a voice coming from the dark.

There is a guy in a booth **WHO** asks, "Who's going on a special adventure tonight?"

And Huey and Dewey point at me and say, "Louie!"

So the guy looks at me and says, "Great! Are you ready?" and I say, "Um, I guess so."

And I get closer and I realize that he is not a person but a super cool robot who looks super-duper real.

And he points to this giant red button in front of a screen, and he says, "Push the button to find out what kind of adventure you're going to have," but I'm nervous, so I don't want to push the button. I mean, yeah, I admit it, I get nervous sometimes, but the other guys are like, "Come on! It's fun! Push the button!" So I push the button and eight words come up on-screen:

YOU ARE ABOUT TO HAVE A GROUNDBREAKING EXPERIENCE!

And everyone goes, "Cool!" but I'm still nervous, and then I pick up the virtual reality glasses, and I ask the guys, "Are you guys going to have an adventure, too?" and they all nod and say stuff like "Yup" and "Right after you," and so I don't want to look scared, so I put the glasses on, and all the lights go out.

HOLY SMOKES, WAS THAT ALL ONE SENTENCE?

I'M getting nervous just listening to you, Louie! Take your time! Breathe! Relax! How is anyone going to understand what you are saying?

Okay, okay, I'll relax.

So I had these glasses on and it was pitch-black and I couldn't see two inches in front of my face. And I decided that maybe this mystery adventure thing wasn't for me, and I started to take the glasses off when I heard a low rumbling coming from what sounded like below the ground.

"WHAT WAS THAT NOISE?" I asked nobody in particular, but I'm not sure they could hear me because all of a sudden there was an ear-splitting CRACK!!!! and the walls of the tent started to rattle, and I realized the one thing I was more afraid of than anything else was about to happen, so I shouted, **"EARTHQUAKE!"** and "EVERYBODY RUN!" and I started to run, but the only problem was that the ground started to split in two right under my feet, meaning my left leg was on one side of the crack, and my right leg was on the other, and I knew I had to jump, and I screamed **"JUMP!"** to myself, I guess, but I wasn't sure which way to jump, and rocks were falling all around me, and I looked down and saw the Earth, ready to swallow up anything in its path, and then, as if that wasn't bad enough, emerging from the giant emptiness, I saw what looked like a twenty-foot tall green goblin or ghost, reaching up for me, and did I mention I hate **GOBLINS**, too?

I THINK EVERYONE HATES GOBLINS.

And the goblin said to me, "Are you enjoying your evening?" and then the goblin said, "I, too, would like to have some fun." And the crack in the floor was getting wider and wider. I knew I would have to jump, otherwise I risked getting split in half! Or falling.

Dewey, which sounds better: getting split in half or falling into a hole in the Earth?

NEITHER SOUNDS GREAT, TO BE HONEST WITH YOU.

I agree.

And then the goblin opened his massive jaws, so it was now or never, and then I jumped, and I landed in a giant river, and I was soaked, and the next thing I knew, something was pulling at my head, and I thought it was the goblin, so I fought back. I fought against the monster, until I heard my brother Huey say, "Louie! Louie! It's us!" And then the next thing I knew, I was looking at my brothers and I was back in the Mystery Tent and the earthquake was over and I was soaking wet.

DO YOU WANT ME TO TAKE IT FROM HERE?

Yes, please. I'm exhausted. Being the narrator is difficult!

I don't blame you.
ME NEITHER.

ANYWAY, LOUIE, YOU WERE STANDING THERE, ALL WET, AND YOU LOOKED AT US LIKE YOU'D JUST SEEN A GHOST.

Which I had.
I thought you said goblin.

Really? You want to question my nightmare?

GUYS! GUYS! CAN WE KEEP GOING?

He always wants to be right!

Anyway . . .

Huey asked Louie, "What happened?"

"It was an earthquake," Louie said, his voice barely above a whisper. "The ground cracked open and I had to jump or be **SWALLOWED** up by a giant green monster."

We all stared at him.

"How did you guys snap me out of it?" Louie asked.

Sophie held up a bucket. "We tried to take the glasses off your face, but you were jumping around like crazy, so we couldn't grab them," she said, handing Louie a small hankie. "Finally we found a bucket of water in the storage closet outside and we **DUMPED** it on you."

Louie stared at us. "The water was in the storage closet?"

Sophie smiled, waving her hands as if she was trying to dismiss the issue. "I'm sure it was fresh and unused!"

In that moment we heard the voice of the cool robot again. "Hey, how was your adventure?"

Louie looked at him. "Horrible! There was a giant earthquake and I almost got swallowed up!"

"Awesome," replied the bot-guy. "This is one of Dr. Z's most **POPULAR** creations and I'm sure he is going to be delighted to hear that you had an amazing time!"

We all looked at each other. "Dr. Z?" I said. "Dr. Z is behind this?"

We all **SCRAMBLED** out of the tent as fast as we could.

Once we had run far enough away and felt safe, Sophie leaned into Hans, my brothers, and me and started whispering. "Okay, you heard it, too. He said that Dr. Z invented the tent. Strange and scary things are happening all over the place!"

"Yeah, first the stuff at the soccer field, and now this!" exclaimed Huey.

"Exactly," she said. "But there's one thing all these episodes have had in common. Or I should say, one person."

We all nodded. **DR. Z**

UM, Dewey? I think the reader gets that by now.

GETS WHAT?

That Dr. Z is up to something and we really need to find out more.

Yeah. The guy is in the middle of everything.

OH. OKAY. WELL, YOU CAN NEVER BE TOO CLEAR.

Right. Got it. Carry on.

Yep, plow ahead.

THANKS SO MUCH, BOTH OF YOU.
I REALLY APPRECIATE THE SUPPORT.

It's nothing.

That's what brothers are for,
am I right?

You are so right.

"So what do you think we should do about Dr. Z?" Louie asked.

"We need to confirm that he is behind this and stop him! We need to figure out two things. How he's doing what he's doing, and why he's doing it. There's only one way to get to the bottom of this whole **MESS**," I said.

All heads turned in my direction. "Tomorrow's the championship game, right?" I asked Hans. He nodded.

I paused for dramatic effect, then lowered my voice.

BECAUSE
I HAVE A PLAN.

CHAPTER 12

The next day at school started out totally normal. We went about our daily classes and tried not to fail gym. When lunch finally came around, we all made our way to the cafeteria. I glanced at the other kids.

Sophie was taking selfies with some of her other friends, as usual.

Meanwhile, Huey and Louie were playing against each other in some video game, which was also something they did all the time.

I could predict what would happen, because it happened every time they **COMPETED**.

It would be fun at first, until it got too *INTENSE*, and then they would end up arguing with each other.

that's how you choose to interpret it. We think it's just a way to exercise our healthy competitive spirits.

Especially when I win.

Which is never.

Which is always.

Never.

Always.

YOU TWO ARE PROVING MY POINT RIGHT NOW, DO YOU REALIZE THAT?

Oh.

Oh.

On any other day, I would have been perfectly happy just to mind my own business, but we had an important **MISSION** coming up.

"Are you guys sure you want to be fooling around like this? We have a **BIG DAY** today," I said.

My brothers were still going at it, so they ignored me, but Sophie glanced up. "We'll be ready to go," she said. "You have nothing to worry about."

I decided to go talk to Hans, who was eating with his soccer buddies.

He saw me coming and stood up. He seemed a little distracted. "What's up?"

"I think there might be something weird going on with my kaleidoscope," I told him. "I opened my bag and it was glowing!"

He looked at him. "That's weird. Are you sure it was the kaleidoscope?"

"I'm positive. Have you ever noticed anything weird with yours?"

Hans shrugged. "Nope."

"I remember thinking there was something strange about this kaleidoscope when we got it," I told him. "The first time I looked through it, I got this weird **DREAMLIKE** feeling, almost like I went into a trance or something."

"Well, you can try to find out more later," Hans said, but I could tell he was still distracted. "We have a big game we need to worry about today, so we have to prepare."

"I'm sure you guys will be great!" I said.

"Yeah." He turned to go back to his friends. "I'll see you at the game."

I nodded. "Yep, you will. But not for **LONG**."

• • •

Okay, so I thought the first game was crazy, but the championship game was on another **LEVEL** entirely!

First of all, there was a marching band there this time. And there was a whole row of food stands, selling everything from sausages to donuts to apple cider.

When we got to the stadium, Hans was on the field with his team. They were warming up by passing the ball back and forth to each other.

Don't forget to say the most important part.

I WON'T.

Drumroll, please . . .

THEY WEREN'T USING HANS'S BALL. WE MADE SURE OF THAT BY TAKING HANS'S BALL AND HIDING IT IN THE BACK OF SOPHIE'S CLOSET AT HOME.

Yay, us!

Meanwhile, the other team was wearing yellow-and-black uniforms, which made it look like a hive of swarming bees.

That reminded me: **I HATE BEES**. And heights. But mostly bees.

Dewey, they know all that already.

Yeah, you're repeating yourself.

SO-RRY!

The other team was also warming up.

Louie leaned over to Sophie. "They look really good." Sophie didn't seem concerned. "Hans and the boys will have everything under control. I'm not worried." I searched the stadium until I found the person I was looking for. After about twenty seconds, I finally spotted him. **DR. Z.**

He was smiling and chatting with some other people. Each team huddled up in a circle and then took the field. The referee blew his **WHISTLE**.

GAME ON

That was our cue to leave.

CHAPTER 13

Everyone was fixated on the game, of course, so Huey, Louie, Sophie, and I were able to **SNEAK** away without anyone noticing.

It took us about fifteen minutes to walk from the soccer stadium to our destination: Dr. Z.'s Toy and Sports Emporium.

It was **CLOSED**, of course.

That was exactly what we wanted. We went around the corner and, luckily, found an open window.

"I'll go through it first," Sophie said. "Then I'll open the back door." Sophie effortlessly slithered through the window, and ten seconds later the back door creaked open.

Sophie motioned for us to come inside.

"Are we sure this is a good idea?" whispered Louie. "That guy is a weirdo. What if this place is full of booby traps or there are some serious dangers? What if we get **CAUGHT?**"

"Yes, it's a good idea. Relax!" Huey answered. "We need to find out what Dr. Z has been up to, and this is the only way."

We were just going to take a look around and **COLLECT**.

That was the plan, anyway.

"Where do you want to start?" Louie asked with a little shake in his voice. "Can we stick together?"

I gave him a little squeeze on the shoulder. "Of course we can stick together. We're a *TEAM*."

"Okay, cool," Louie said, but right between the words "okay" and "cool," Huey veered off down the hall.

Louie didn't like that one bit. "Huey!" he whispered fiercely. "Where are you going?"

"Downstairs, where Dr. Z said his *LABORATORY* was," Huey called. "He tried to take our attention off this place too quickly the other day. So that's where we should start!"

Huey had rounded the corner by then and was out of sight.

"You coming?" he called back to us, but then we heard what sounded like a weird **SLURP**, and then we heard Huey make a noise that sounded like "Mamachuca Gargeebargee," and then we heard absolutely nothing.

Mamachuca Gargeebargee?

> YES. MAMACHUCA GARGEEBARGEE.

Cool. Just making sure.

Sophie, Louie, and I looked at each other. "That's what happens when you break away from the **GANG**," hissed Louie.

"We'd better go down there and see what happened," I said.

Sophie nodded, and after about ten long seconds, Louie finally agreed as well.

Stop making me sound like such a scaredy-cat!

> You ARE a scaredy-cat!

So what? They don't need to know that!

> BUT THEY KIND OF DO, SINCE THAT'S PART OF THE STORY.

In every other sentence?

I'LL TRY NOT TO.

Thank you. By the way, just hearing this story all over again is filling me with fear and trembling. But don't mind me. Please continue.

We headed quickly to the top of the stairs.

"We have to find him!" said Sophie, putting her foot on the first step.

We started going down the stairs pretty slowly.

"What if it's a *TRAP*?" I whispered.

"A what?" Louie asked.

But before I could repeat what I'd said, we heard the same slurping sound we'd heard before.

Then the stairs VANISHED underneath our feet, and we were suddenly on a slimy slide that swirled us down, down, down, into total DARKNESS.

The air got colder and colder, and we must have been on that slick, slippery ride for

a full ninety seconds before we **TUMBLED** onto some sort of soft, squishy substance that smelled like soaked socks.

We got up, brushed ourselves off, and tried to look around before realizing it was very dark. "It stinks down here," Louie said, stating the obvious. As our eyes adjusted to the darkness, the first thing we saw was Huey, standing two feet away from us.

"HUEY!" exclaimed Louie, but it quickly became clear that Huey was otherwise occupied. He was staring up at a big shelf, high up on the wall. It had a cage on it. **SOMETHING** was moving inside the cage, but it was too dark to see what it was.

IT'S ALIVE. WHATEVER IS IN THERE, IT'S ALIVE.

"I can't see!" Louie said, frustrated. "Are there any lights down here?" I glanced around.

"I think I see a couple switches over there. Should I try them?"

"Yes!" Louie said, and "No!" Sophie said at the exact same time.

I listened to my brother, which might have been a **MISTAKE**. I flipped the switches to the on position, and we immediately heard a low rumbling sound while a bright white light practically blinded us.

The light came from a rack of fluorescent bulbs across the ceiling. The low rumbling came from a **GIANT** machine in the middle of the room. It whirred to life, blinking and buzzing.

It was covered with red and blue wires, which were **SHOOTING** off sparks; wrapping around the side of the machine was a giant test tube filled with thick, boiling green liquid.

"Turn it back off!" Huey said, and I did. I reached for the switches again and flipped one, hoping it was for the machine. Luckily it was, and it shut off with a groan.

Sophie said, "The stairs were a trick to get us down here. A *TRAP*." She laughed a little sadly. "And, uh, it worked." We explored the machine a little more, trying to find out exactly what it did.

"Great," Louie said sarcastically. Then he pointed up at the shelf, where the cage was. "I still want to know what's in that cage, though."

We all peered up, but the cage was too high. All we could see were **SHADOWS** moving around inside it, and we heard a soft scuttling sound.

"Maybe it's bees," I said, remembering the massive hive Huey and I had seen when we had our nightmare in the woods, or whatever it was. Huey shook his head. "Bees don't scuttle. They buzz."

"Good point," I said.

I THINK WE SHOULD GO. I'M SCARED. THERE, I ADMIT IT. I'M SCARED AND I WANT TO GO.

"Can I tell you something?" Huey said. "I'm a little scared myself." I was about to admit that I, too, was a little frightened when the LIGHTS suddenly went out again.

At that point, it was official: I was definitely scared.

"Wh-what's happening?" stuttered Louie. "Who did that?"

"I DID," someone behind us said.

The four of us looked at each other, but none of us turned around to see who it was.

Because we all recognized that **VOICE**.

CHAPTER
14

A faint purple light suddenly clicked on over the door. (It reminded me of the purple lights that were in the Mystery Tent.) It made a hissing sound that was very loud in the silence.

Peering through the dimness, I could barely make out the form of Dr. Z standing at the top of the steps in his white coat, with a big smile on his face.

"Why, this is certainly a *PLEASANT SURPRISE!*" he said gleefully "I love company! To what do I owe the honor?"

My tongue was *FROZEN* in my mouth, but somehow Sophie managed to speak.

"We—we thought you were at the game," she said.

"Oh, I was, I was. And what a game it was! Two excellent teams, very evenly matched," Dr. Z said.

He started walking down the stairs, slowly.

"But then I thought, 'Where are my young *FRIENDS* from America? The ones who so impressed me when I first met them, and with whom I became friends at the honorary dinner the other night.'"

"You–you mean the night of the *EARTHQUAKE* that almost *SWALLOWED* me up?" stammered Louie.

The professor frowned. "I don't remember that."

"Louie could have fallen into that giant black hole and been eaten by the ghostly goblin," I *WHISPERED*.

By then the professor had reached the bottom of the stairs. "Not really," he said. "You see, what I've conjured up over the past few days have just been fun, silly warm-ups. A prelude to the *MAIN EVENT*."

He flipped the same switch I had touched previously, and the machine revved up once again.

"And today *IS THE MAIN EVENT*."

"We need to go," Sophie said. "We have to get back to the game."

"So soon?" asked Dr. Z. "We're finally getting to know each other."

Sophie hesitated, then suddenly sprinted up the stairs to the door. But Dr. Z pressed a button high on the wall, and the door bolted shut with a loud *CLANK!*

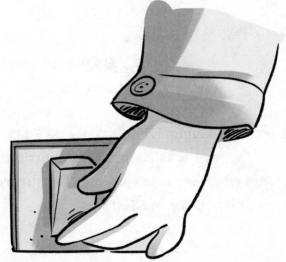

HELP! SOMEBODY, HELP!

But it was no use. We were trapped.

"Now, where were we?" asked Dr. Z. "Oh yes, I imagine you all have some questions?"

"**Why** are you doing all this?" Huey asked.

"**How** are you doing all this?" Louie asked.

"**WHAT'S** in that cage up there?" I asked.

Dr. Z laughed, but it was a *DARK* laugh.

"Wow, I was right, such inquisitive youngsters! And whatever is in that cage is a surprise that you'll meet if you try to *ESCAPE*."

He sat down in a big red chair that was next to the **WEIRD** machine, and fiddled with some knobs as he talked. "As for the why, you're all aware that I grew up here but then left a long time ago. And perhaps you're also aware that I've become quite an accomplished inventor in the intervening years. But I believe you're unaware of **WHY** I moved away in the first place."

The machine with the test tube filled with green goo started to rumble **LOUDER**.

"I have always been fascinated with **FEAR**," continued Dr. Z. "It is an extraordinary emotion. In a way, it is the most **POWERFUL** thing on Earth. Fear drives everything. I know this firsthand, because as a child, I myself was consumed by fear. Everything frightened me: being alone, being in a crowd, animals, germs, the dark, getting hurt, playing games—you name it. I lived my life being **SCARED** of everything."

"So what happened?" Sophie asked.

Dr. Z was gazing over our heads, as if he was looking at the memory itself.

"Well, as it turns out, being a child who is *AFRAID* of everything puts a damper on your social life. It was hard to be friends with other children when they were all enjoying the scary movie, or laughing at the small insect, or enjoying a sleepover, or roughhousing with one another, and you were the one *FRIGHTENED* out of your wits."

"Well," I said, "then why are you scaring *US?*"

Dr. Z glared at me. "I'll get there." His eyes *GLAZED* over again, and he went back to his memory.

"Eventually, my parents sent me away, to a tiny school on a tiny road in a tiny town in the middle of nowhere, where I learned to deal with my difficulties. It was there that I started to understand the *POWER* that fear has over all of us.

AND WITH POWER COMES CONTROL.

I realized if you could make the people around you frightened and fearful, you could then gain control over them very easily. So I started working on how

I COULD SCARE THE WHOLE WORLD.

He smiled a **SHIVERY** smile, and his voice dropped to an eerie **WHISPER**.

"Because if you can scare the world, you can control the world." Whatever he was doing, it was working right then, because we were **MIGHTY SCARED**.

WELL, YOUR PLAN WON'T WORK, BECAUSE WE ALREADY DESTROYED THE EVIL BALL YOU GAVE HANS. AND WE SAVED LOUIE. AND WE ESCAPED FROM THE TENT.

"Very impressive, young lady," said Dr. Z in a **WEIRDLY** gentle voice. "Perhaps you are all just too clever for me. Perhaps I should just throw my **SPECIAL FORMULA** out with the rest of the day's trash."

"W—what formula?"

stammered Louie.

"And why here, and why us?" added Huey.

"WHAT DID WE EVER DO TO YOU?"

"SO MANY QUESTIONS! I really am impressed with your curiosity."

Dr. Z took a **REMOTE** out of his pocket and stood up.

"Here in Berlin was where it all began for me, and where I learned the importance of fear. So when I was ready to start testing my **EXPERIMENTS**, I decided to come back to the place where it began, to chase away my own personal **DEMONS**. Too bad you decided to visit Berlin right now and get **INVOLVED**."

By the way, whose idea was it to get involved, anyway?

I think it was yours.

Really? I think it was yours.

IT WAS ALL OF OURS! NOW HUSH.

Aye, aye, captain.

CHAPTER
15

Dr. Z pressed a button on the remote, and all of a sudden, the machine started to whir and rumble. Slowly, the **GREEN LIQUID** started to flow down the test tube and into pipes that snaked up into the wall and somewhere beyond.

"After my inventions gained the respect of millions around the world, my hometown was ready to welcome me back with open arms. But they didn't realize I had a plan all along–a plan to wreak **REVENGE** on this town that had humiliated and discarded me all those years ago."

Dr. Z smiled, baring his **YELLOW TEETH**.

"You see, I kept one of my inventions a **SECRET**. This green liquid in these tubes here is actually what I call **THE NIGHTMARE FORMULA**.

"When I inject this green **LIQUID** into a physical object, such as a soccer ball or a pair of virtual reality glasses, and a person comes into contact with that item, the brain is **TRIGGERED** to imagine an experience of one's greatest **PERSONAL FEAR**, creating such terror that it renders them immobile. In their head, they are going through a *HORRIFYING EXPERIENCE*, but in reality, nothing is happening to them. It's all simply *FEAR*."

"Someone will figure out a way to stop you," Huey said. "Not everyone is scared of something. Some people aren't afraid of anything."

"Well, now," said Dr. Z, "I'm afraid that's not quite true. *EVERYONE* is frightened of something. Take you children, for example. You will recall the *KALEIDO-SCOPE* I gave you?"

I certainly did. "The one with the weird patterns?"

"That's the one. When I gave it to you, do you remember falling into somewhat of a *TRANCE?*"

We all nodded slowly.

"Well, that's because there is a special trick of **HYPNOSIS** within the refracting light inside that kaleidoscope, making you admit your fears, so I could use the infor- mation to plan my **REVENGE**."

We all stared at him. Could that possibly be true?

Dr. Z looked at Huey. "You are afraid of **SNAKES**."

He looked at me. "For you, it's **BEES**."

He looked at Louie. "And you, **EARTHQUAKES**. I just threw that green goblin in for fun."

Dr. Z turned his evil attention to Sophie. "And you, **MY DEAR?** Would you like me to tell everyone what it is that you're most **AFRAID OF?**"

The color drained from Sophie's face. "Or perhaps you'd like to tell us?" said Dr. Z. But Sophie could only shake her head.

Dr. Z laughed.

"Oh, come now! You children come to my store, uninvited, trying to **DISRUPT** the events that I've been planning for many years. The least you can do is answer one simple question."

He lowered his voice to a **SCARY** rumble.

"What are you afraid of, my dear?"

Her voice was barely above a whisper.

"SPIDERS."

Dr. Z joyfully clapped his hands together. "Oh, my goodness! What a wonderful coincidence!"

He looked at the remote he still had in his hands and pressed a button.

The high shelf—the one with the cage on it—began to lower itself. Sophie's lower lip was trembling.

"Please don't do this," she said.

A big smile crossed Dr. Z's face.

"I'm sorry, my dear, but your friends did ask what was in the cage, did they not? And what kind of host would I be if I didn't answer my guests' questions?"

"YOU'RE NOT GOING TO GET AWAY WITH THIS!" Huey shouted, probably just to make himself feel better. **"WE'LL FIGURE OUT A WAY TO STOP YOU!"**

You guys gotta admit that was a pretty brave moment for me.

Fine, it was brave. What do you want, a medal?

Actually, yes, I'd love a medal. Why, do you have one?

Absolutely not.

The scuttling got louder as the shelf continued to lower. The cage was filled with spiders of all shapes and sizes, crawling over each other, seeming like they wanted nothing more than to escape and do what spiders do: scare people half to death.

I pointed with a trembling hand. "Th-th-those spiders are real," I stammered. "You said it was all in our *IMAGINATIONS*." Dr. Z shrugged.

"Well, rules are meant to be broken, are they not?" His eyes narrowed to little slits. "Remember, I said this was the main event. We're playing for keeps this time."

"Please, no," Sophie said. "Anything but the spiders. We promise not to tell anyone what you're doing. Just no spiders, I *BEG* you."

"What is it you want?" Huey asked as we all continued to stare at the descending cage. "Do you have some other plan?"

"Ah, yes," Dr. Z said.

Then he laughed—a maniacal, *TERRIFYING LAUGH*.

"I've been working very hard, perfecting a way to turn my *NIGHTMARE FORMULA* into a fine mist that I can release into the air.

"That way, everyone who breathes it in will have their own terrifying experiences. Eventually, I will manage to paralyze the entire population.

AND THE WORLD WILL BE MINE TO DO WITH IT WHAT I WILL."

He rose from the red chair and pointed at the green sludge, which was continuing to drip slowly out of the machine and into pipes in the wall and underneath the floor.

"These pipes run all the way underground to the **NEW SOCCER** field I just built, where the liquid will seep into the grass. First the players will be affected. Then, when the spectators run onto the field to help them, they, too, will be bedeviled by the **NIGHTMARE FORMULA**. It promises to be quite a sight."

He paused, relishing the thought.

"How do you think you'll possibly get away with it?" I asked, aghast.

"We will tell everyone what we know!" exclaimed Huey.

Dr. Z leaned into him. "Who do you think they will believe, a couple of kids, or one of the most **DISTINGUISHED** scientists in the whole country? And no matter what, you first need to get out of here . . . alive!"

A look of **HORROR** crossed Huey's, Louie's and Sophie's faces, and I'm sure mine as well.

"YOU CAN'T DO THAT!" I yelled. **"THESE PEOPLE ARE INNOCENT! THEY HAD NOTHING TO DO WITH YOUR FEARS WHEN YOU LIVED HERE! YOU CAN'T JUST TERRORIZE THEM!"**

"Is anyone really **INNOCENT?**" asked Dr. Z.

And it was then that Louie—nervous, scared, lazy Louie—screamed **"AARRRGHGHHH!"** and charged full steam right at Dr. Z.

This is one of my favorite parts.

Of course it is.

Please continue, Dewey, and take your time.

We all stared at Louie, wondering where this **BRAVERY** had come from. Even Dr. Z was surprised.

When Louie hit him, Dr. Z lost his balance and stumbled while losing his grip on the remote, which Louie was able to catch right before it hit the ground.

Dr. Z looked **SHOCKED** at what had happened.

"That's mine," he hissed.

Louie threw the remote control to Huey, who caught it and then immediately dropped it, as if it was made out of worms.

"I don't want it," Huey said. "I might push the wrong button."

"GIVE IT TO ME!" Dr. Z lunged for the gadget, but Sophie got to it first.

"Which button stops the green sludge?!" she cried.

Dr. Z's eyes became even more *EVIL*.

"And why would I ever do that?" he said.

Sophie stared down at the remote control, trying to figure out what to do.

I ran to Sophie, as I was feeling left out and I wanted to do something brave and heroic. Without giving it a second thought, I grabbed the **REMOTE**.

I THINK I KNOW WHICH ONE IS RIGHT!

Bad move.

Yeah. Super bad.

As soon as I pushed the button, the cage with all the spiders started to rattle and shake.

Then the cage door **OPENED**.

Meanwhile, the green goo kept on pulsing through the pipes.

Dr. Z suddenly went from angry to very, very **GLAD**. "Oops, someone's not as smart at they thought!" he chirped, clapping his hands together in demented joy. I suddenly felt about **TWO INCHES TALL**.

"You . . . I . . ."

Dr. Z looked gleeful. "Yes?"

His cackle echoed through the room as spiders poured out of the cage.

It was like watching a **HORROR MOVIE** in slow motion. The spiders started crawling over the table, the machine, and the chair–all heading in Sophie's direction. Her eyes **BULGED** out of her head, and she was so scared her legs wouldn't move.

The green sludge moved through the pipes faster and faster, beginning its journey toward the soccer field, while the machine turned red and started throwing off **SPARKS**, ripping the wires.

The laboratory crackled and hissed as the light bulbs **BURNED OUT** one by one.

Soon it would be completely dark except for the sparks shooting out from the torn wires. The three of us were looking around, trying to find something to stop the spiders or Dr. Z.

"TODAY WE SETTLE THE SCORE!" thundered Dr. Z.

I was reminded of the board game called Settle The Score that Dr. Z had shown us the second time we visited the store.

Wait a second, I thought.

His store. The kaleidoscope. **FEARS.**

Then I saw some cables lying on the floor not far from us. And that's when I had an **IDEA**.

"You know something, you guys?" I said. "Dr. Z thinks he's such an expert on discovering what people's fears are. Well, guess what? I think I know what his fear is."

The mad scientist glowered at me. "Oh, yeah? What's that?"

I smirked. "Being outsmarted by a bunch of kids."

"That's absurd!"

Dr. Z scrambled to his feet.

"I AM THE SMARTEST PERSON IN ANY ROOM I'M IN. ESPECIALLY WHEN THE ROOM I'M IN IS FILLED WITH CLUELESS YOUNGSTERS LIKE YOURSELVES."

I looked at Huey, and he backed me up, also noticing the cables I was looking at. "Dewey's right," he said.

"And you know something else? Your fear is not only being **OUTSMARTED** by kids. You're also scared of people finding out that you're not scary at all. You're just a mean, bitter old man with nothing better to do."

"That's **NONSENSE!**" the mad scientist sputtered.

"I'm not scared of you," Louie said. He looked at me. "Are you?"

"Nope," I said. I looked at Huey. "Are you?"

"Nope," Huey said. He looked at Sophie. "Are you?"

Sophie, who was still basically paralyzed by the spiders, tried to shake her head, but it barely moved.

Poor Sophie, she was so scared. Hey, Huey, I bet you wanted to hug her and make her feel better right about then, huh?

I think the readers would appreciate it if you minded your own business right about now, Louie.

Well, I think the readers like hearing about your crush on Sophie.

154

I THINK THE READERS WOULD ACTUALLY PREFER IT IF YOU BOTH STOPPED BICKERING.

Why do you think that? People love bickering!

No they don't.

Yes they do.

CAN YOU GUYS DRAW A PICTURE OF ME ROLLING MY EYES RIGHT ABOUT NOW?

"NONE OF US ARE SCARED OF YOU," I said. "And that's why I'm not scared of your laboratory, either, or your illusions, or your spiders, or your stupid machine. I'm not even scared of that other cage."

"What other cage?" Dr. Z demanded, frowning.

I pointed at the ceiling. "The one way up there, that you haven't lowered yet."

Dr. Z looked irritated. "What on **EARTH** are you talking about?" He craned his neck upward to look—which was when Huey and I grabbed the **CABLES** and pulled them, running around Dr. Z to try to trap him.

And at that moment, the last light bulb also went out and we were in complete darkness. We were only able to get a little bit of visibility with the fluorescence of the *GREEN SLIME*.

"AHHH!" Dr. Z cried. "WHAT ON EARTH ARE YOU DOING?" Then he tripped and fell backward into his machine, which groaned, sputtered to a stop, and keeled over right on top of his leg, splashing the floor and walls with the green slime.

"YEEEEEE—OUCH!" he bellowed.

Louie cackled. "Looks like you should be scared of these kids!"

"Yeah!" added Huey.

"But hey—it's not like we outsmarted him or anything, right, you guys? You just fell for the oldest *TRICK* in the book!"

"YOU'LL PAY FOR THIS!" Dr. Z thundered.

Then he tried to get up, but he couldn't free his leg from under the machine.

He was stuck!

HEYYYY!

"Now's our chance!" said Huey.

"Let's get out of here!"

"We just need to get away from the spiders and reach that **SWITCH** on the wall!" said Louie, moving toward the door at the top of the stairs.

The spiders were crawling all over the place, but I actually kind of like spiders. And hey, they don't call me Daring Dewey for nothing!

No one calls you that.

SOME PEOPLE DO!

No one I know does.
Most people call you Silly–Dilly Dewey.

Yeah. That's what I call you.

Well, I was **DARING** right then! Because I climbed over the spiders and tried to reach the stairs and Louie to push him up so he could hit the switch.

But just as I was about to reach him, I felt something grip my **LEG**.

It was Dr. Z's hand. He had freed himself from the machine and seemed very angry.

"You won't get away with this," he hissed.

He yanked my leg, and I fell to the ground beside him. I tried to get up but immediately slipped back down; the slime kept pouring out of the machine, making the floor incredibly **SLIPPERY**.

"Get your hands off me!" I cried, but he started dragging me toward the machine.

"You won't last long. You are all covered with the formula, and you'll soon experience the most terrifying nightmares of your young life," Dr. Z said. **"THAT'S WHAT YOU GET FOR TRYING TO TRICK ME!"**

I started feeling dizzy and seeing the walls move and the floor shake.

Then, out of the corner of my eye, I saw Huey and Louie sneaking up behind Dr. Z. They reached down and pulled Dr. Z's long **LAB COAT** up over his head.

Suddenly, he couldn't see a thing.

"WHAT'S THAT?" he hollered. **"WHAT'S GOING ON? WHO'S THERE?"**

He reached up with his free arm to grab his coat, but Huey and Louie held on for dear life while trying to tie him up, until he finally let go of my leg.

The second he did that, I **LEAPT** up, ran toward the bottom of the stairs—where Huey joined me—jumped on Huey's shoulder, and pressed the switch, unlocking the door. We all charged up after Huey and sprinted out of the basement only to realize that Sophie was still down there, unable to move, as if she was stuck in **QUICKSAND**! But she wasn't.

She was stuck in fear. And we were all starting to feel more and more the effect of the green formula on our minds.

We had to get out of there immediately.

"I'm coming back for you!" I called to Sophie.

But just as I got to her, Dr. Z finally managed to free himself from his coat. I **PULLED** Sophie away just as the first spider started crawling up her leg.

"Thank y–you," she managed to stammer.

We clambered up the stairs as fast as we could, hoping to lock Dr. Z in the basement, but he was right behind us.

He stuck his foot in the door before we could **SLAM** it in his face. I could hear him cackling.

That was our cue to **RUN**.

CHAPTER 16

Dr. Z was still screaming as we sprinted toward the front doors of his slimy, scary store.

There was a sudden hissing sound, and the hallway began to fill with a green haze.

"IT'S TOO LATE!" he roared! *"I'VE RELEASED THE MIST INSIDE THE STORE! YOU'RE BREATHING IT IN RIGHT NOW! BE PREPARED TO BE AS SCARED AS YOU'VE EVER BEEN IN YOUR LIVES!"*

I glanced behind me to make sure my brothers were still there.

"HUEY!" I screamed. **"LOUIE! WHERE ARE YOU GUYS!?!?"**

I heard Huey's voice, but it sounded far away. **"WE'RE HERE! WE'RE COMING!"**

I turned around again, but all I saw was that ghostly **GREEN GOBLIN**, with three yellowish-purple eyes blinking wildly. The mist was starting to work.

The goblin was gaining on me. I ran faster.

"You children are being very rude houseguests!" Dr. Z yelled. "You haven't even allowed me to offer you anything to eat!" And right at that moment, a **GIANT CABBAGE** descended from the ceiling and blocked my path.

Man, did it smell yucky.

"EEEEEWWWW!" I screamed, untangling myself from the cabbage as if it was a man-eating plant. "This is **DISGUSTING!**"

Finally, I found Sophie and my brothers, and we got ourselves out of the store, with Dr. Z still chasing us. It turned out he had one last trick up his sleeve: he threw a Frisbee at Louie. "Hey, kid!" he yelled. "Catch!"

And before Louie realized what was happening, he caught the **FRISBEE**.

Not a smart move.

Yeah, we all got that, thanks!

We all looked at each other.

"Uh–oh," Louie said.

The Frisbee began glowing and turning different colors. Louie dropped it immediately as we started sprinting back toward the field, but the damage was done. Between the mist and the Frisbee, all the creatures we'd seen in our various waking **NIGHTMARES** came back to haunt us.

We turned the corner and there was the swarm of bees, buzzing around our arms and landing on our faces.

The **GIANT SNAKE MONSTER**, which jumped out of a tree, chased us until Huey had the amazing idea of hopping on a city bus.

That was great until we took our seats on the bus, looked around, and realized everyone else on the bus was a **LIZARD**.

That explained the lizards.

We jumped off the bus and ran down the street, which began to split underneath our feet.

Boulders started falling from the sky as the ground splintered and groaned.

"ANOTHER EARTHQUAKE!" moaned Louie. **"JUST LIKE AT THE MYSTERY TENT!"**

A thought occurred to me, and I stopped running for a second. "Why are we so scared of all this stuff?" I said. "We know it's not real, right?"

But just as I said that, a **BOULDER** missed my head by about three inches.

"RUN!!!!" I hollered.

Huey pointed to the sky. "Look!"

A **BLACK CLOUD** had formed, in the shape of Dr. Z's head.

"Run as fast as you can!" said the cloud head. "But you won't get away!"

But we DID get away, because Huey—

Remember, I'm the heroic one.

Yeah, they got that.

Anyway, Huey grabbed a tree branch that had fallen, and quickly placed it across the cracked street, providing a bridge for us.

As soon as we made it to the other side, we picked up the branch so Dr. Z, whose human form was still right behind us, couldn't make it **ACROSS**.

"Hahaha!" Louie yelled. "You created this earthquake, but you can't catch us!"

Except somehow Dr. Z walked right across the **CRACKED STREET**.

We stared at him, and he grinned.

"I invented the **NIGHTMARE FORMULA**, remember? I made myself immune!" he explained.

Dr. Z was gaining on us as we rounded one last corner and finally made it to the field.

The mist cleared, and our illusions faded away, which just meant we could see the field extremely clearly. It was in utter **CHAOS**.

The grass on the field glowed a **_BIZARRE_** shade of green, just like the goo in Dr. Z's machine.

The players were all screaming, running around in circles, and flailing their arms in the air, having their own **_IMAGINARY NIGHTMARES_**.

I heard one kid yelling about not knowing how to swim, and saw another kid screaming because he thought he was dangling out of an airplane and he hated heights. Yet another player was hollering that he wasn't going to eat his peas, because peas made him vomit. And the **_SPECTATORS_** who had run onto the field were busy dealing with their own terrifying illusions.

Sophie pointed and exclaimed, "Look at poor Hans!" He was near the goal on one end of the field, spinning around wildly in **CIRCLES**.

"Oh, man," Huey said. "We need to do something." But Louie shook his head.

"If we run out there, our own nightmares will come back. We have to think of something else."

He was right.

As we tried to figure out what to do, we heard a familiar voice behind us.

Of course it was Dr. Z, surveying the success of his evil-doing.

Chapter 17

Life can be so scary sometimes," he said with an evil grin on his face. "Don't you agree?"

"You're a terrible person," Sophie said.

Dr. Z bowed. "Thank you."

We stood there **HELPLESSLY**, knowing that we couldn't run onto the field, because then we would touch the poisonous grass and be completely useless.

Sophie suddenly slapped her forehead, the way they do in cartoons sometimes. "Hey, wait a second! I remember the one thing that can **REVERSE** the curse!"

"You mean the **NIGHTMARE FORMULA?**" Louie whispered.

"Yup," Sophie said, keeping her voice down and starting to walk away from Dr. Z.

"**WATER.**"

"Hey, that's right," said Huey. "water!"

We kept walking away while Dr. Z was distracted and gloating in what appeared to be his success.

"She's absolutely right," I said. "Every time the formula affected someone, we've been able to stop it with water. And we're going to do it again. There's a sprinkler system on this field. We just need to find it!"

"Dewey and Louie, you guys take the left side of the field," Huey said. "Sophie and I will take the right."

We spread out, **SPRINTING** all around the field, checking under every bench and behind the scoreboard, but there was no sign of a sprinkler system.

Then I remembered that crazy practice, when Hans and a few other players on the team went into the nightmares. The coaches had been busy working on something closed up in a small gated area near the parking lot, where they must've kept all the tools and extra equipment.

Maybe the control panel for the sprinklers was in there as well.

Louie and I ran up to an extremely tall metal fence, but the gate was locked. There was a big metal box in the ground that said **"WATER SYSTEMS"** on it.

"This is it!" I said, and I looked around, trying to find Sophie and Huey. They were running toward us.

"It's here!" I shouted at them, waving my arms.

"We need to find a way to get inside," Sophie said, looking at us.

But just as I opened my mouth, a familiar shadow appeared on the shed. "And why exactly do you need to get in there?" Dr. Z asked, looking at us suspiciously.

"WE KNOW HOW TO STOP YOU!" I screamed.

They all stared at me in disbelief.

Why do you always have to talk? Seriously!

Yeah, can't you learn to keep your mouth shut?

Dr. Z got closer, and his eyes got darker and darker. "And what exactly makes you think that?"

Sophie grabbed my hand.

"And what exactly makes you think that we are going to tell you?" She stuck out her **TONGUE**, mocking Dr. Z. "You'll have to catch us first!" And then she darted away, pulling me with her while Dr. Z chased us, enraged.

"You little..." he yelled, furious.

"YOU AND YOUR FRIENDS WILL NEVER GET OUT OF THE NIGHTMARE!"

This was the moment!

Louie and Huey went back to try to find a way to open the gate.

But the **LOCK** wouldn't open. There was no other option: they had to climb the fence to get inside.

"I'll go," said Huey. "Just push me as high as you can, and be ready to **CATCH ME** if I fall."

Huey started climbing to the top, and Louie kept his eyes on him. "You're almost there!" Louie shouted up to Huey. "Just go over the fence and then jump!"

Yeah, nice suggestion, by the way! It was really dangerous!

I thought you were the heroic one!

You made it, so stop complaining!

Anyway, Huey reached the top, jumped, and was in! At the same time, they heard Sophie and me **SCREAM**. Dr. Z had cornered us and was pushing us to walk into the field and plunge into our nightmares again. "Go!" Huey said. "I can manage from here."

Louie mustered all the **COURAGE** he could and ran toward Dr. Z to try to save his friend and his brother, hoping that the water was going to be turned on before everyone was lost, us included.

Louie grabbed an extra goal net that was abandoned on the ground, and tried to catch the crazy scientist with it.

Meanwhile, Sophie and I noticed what Louie was trying to do and turned to Dr. Z to **DISTRACT** him once more. Right when Louie launched the net at him, the sprinklers started dousing the field and water was coming from every direction. **HUEY HAD DONE IT!**

"SWEEET!" I said to myself.

The grass started going back to its normal color, and the **GREEN GOOP** dissolved until there wasn't any left. At the same time, all the people on the field stopped.

We ran around him with the net, doing our best to secure him. We finally trapped him *TIGHTLY* enough in the net that his arms and legs were completely tangled and immobile.

"NOOOOO! IT'S IMPOSSIBLE!" he shouted.

"Let me go! You little scoundrels!"

It took almost two full minutes, but finally the glowing had ceased, replaced **MAGICALLY** with its normal color.

While everyone started to feel better as they walked off the field, they were still extremely confused about what had happened.

The mayor and Sophie's aunt and uncle ran to us to make sure we were all okay. When they got closer and saw Dr. Z tied up like a **GERMAN SAUSAGE**, they stared at us in disbelief.

"Well, what is going on here?" the mayor asked.

"It's quite a story, but we might need some time to explain." Huey said, joining our group. "The most important thing is that we captured the culprit behind all the madness that's been going on." And then, pointing at himself, he added smugly, "And I saved the day by turning the water on!"

You're welcome, world.

Huey! You did a great thing! But why do you always have to brag and ask everyone to love you? Jeez, what kind of hero are you?

Sorry, Louie, you're absolutely right. I take it back. But climbing the high fence and then turning on the water was pretty awesome, right? You gotta admit?

Sheesh. You need to learn how to be the strong, silent type.

Strong and silent. Got it. Carry on, Dewey.

RELEASE ME! RELEASE ME THIS INSTANT!

Dr. Z was still flopping around like a caught fish. "I'm afraid we can't do that," Sophie said. "Release me!" sputtered Dr. Z.

"I demand you set me free!" His desperate eyes found the mayor. "Madame Mayor, please! This is all a giant misunderstanding! It was simply an experiment that went terribly wrong!"

Mayor Klopp looked utterly confused. "What on Earth are you talking about? An **EXPERIMENT?** You promised to build us beautiful fields, and instead you had everyone running around completely terrified!"

Dr. Z stared at the mayor for a few moments, then turned his gaze to Sophie. "I can't believe all it took was water to completely foil my *FORMULA*..." he said while the police arrived and began handcuffing him.

"It most certainly was," Sophie said.

I walked over to Dr. Z and got as close as I could to his face.

"I guess you're not quite as **SMART** as everyone thinks."

Dr. Z stared back at me **VICIOUSLY**.

"We'll see about that."

The mad scientist looked at my brothers and me, and his eyes narrowed in a cold gaze. "If these three busybodies hadn't come to our town and stuck their noses into our **AFFAIRS**," he sneered, "everything would have gone exactly according to plan."

Hans, who had joined us around the handcuffed scientist, stepped forward. "You're absolutely right," he told Dr. Z. Then he turned to us. "And for that, we will be forever **GRATEFUL** to our new friends." Hans pulled us and Sophie into a giant hug.

Sophie gave us each a kiss on the cheek. "You guys were great!" she said.

"Almost as great as you," Louie said.

She grinned. "**ALMOST**, but not quite."

There was one last thing to do: play the actual game. Hans's team won 2 to 1, with Hans getting an assist on the second goal. It was nice that he won, but you know what? It suddenly wasn't all that important.

What was important was that our friends were happy, the town was saved, a bad guy had been caught, **AND WE HAD HELPED!**

After all, we weren't just Huey, Dewey, and Louie, the silly brothers from **DUCKBURG**.

We were International Student Ambassadors, too!

After the crazy business with **Dr. Z,** we stayed in Berlin for almost two more months, but nothing nearly as exciting happened.

What about the time Louie petted that dachshund and it nearly bit his hand off?

that wasn't my fault. The owner said the dog was having a bad day.

Whatever you need to tell yourself, Louie.

Or what about that time when Huey got super carsick on the way to the castle and couldn't join us on the awesome tour?

Not my fault there were so many winding roads!

No one else threw up!

I can't help it if I have a delicate stomach.

Like I was saying, nothing else happened that was nearly as exciting as the **STRANGE CAPER** with Dr. Z and his Nightmare Formula.

On the morning we were leaving Germany, we were in the middle of brushing our teeth when Frau Keller came into our room with a **BRIGHT** smile on her face.

"Guess what?" she exclaimed. "We've got one last appointment for you."

We all looked at each other. "You do?"

"YEP!" said Sophie, barging into the room.

"We're going to the city hall for a special going-away party!"

The party was so great, and it was all for us!

And we got the best surprise ever–and boy, they must have known what would make us happy, because they delivered it:

A CHOCOLATE–FONDUE FOUNTAIN!!!! AAAAAAHHH!!!

I wanted to swim in it.

I totally **DID** swim in it.

Ewwww! no you didn't.

We had the best time at the party, spending time laughing with Hans, Sophie, and our other friends we made in the months there.

Finally, it was time to go back to the Kellers' house, where Sophie and Hans helped us pack up our stuff, and waited with us for the taxi.

But we didn't talk very much. It was almost as if no one was quite sure what to say. Finally, there was a carhorn outside.

We hugged Herr and Frau Keller goodbye first. Then we turned to Hans. "It was really cool meeting you," Huey told him as Louie and I nodded. "We're sure you're going to be a famous soccer player someday."

"Thank you all for saving me," Hans said. "I will never forget any of you."

That left **SOPHIE**.

Louie was shy, so he didn't say anything, but he did give her a **BIG HUG**. I said, "I'm sure we will see you again, very soon," and Sophie nodded.

Huey stepped up and looked at Sophie for what must have been ten seconds. Then he said, "You are the first girl I've ever loved."

Hahahahhahahahahahaha
You are the first girl I've ever loved!

I most certainly, absolutely, definitely didn't even come CLOSE to saying that.

Fine. What you actually said was "It was really nice getting to know you."

Correct.

Maybe you didn't say it.
But you were THINKING it.

Maybe.

So we got ready to leave Germany, with some **SCARY** memories and many **WONDERFUL** friends, ready to see what the rest of our **AMAZING** yearlong adventure had to offer.

It promised to be full of new and exciting adventures, although hopefully not quite as exciting!

And you know what?

We probably weren't going to go to any **TOY STORES** for a while.

EPILOGUE

SOUNDS LIKE THE PERFECT ENDING, RIGHT?

Well, not exactly. I have one last thing to tell you.

After we got to the airport and checked in, we were hanging out in the lounge with Mr. Scholl, fooling around with our phones and eating jelly donuts—which believe it or not, in Berlin are called **BERLINERS!**

Suddenly, Mr. Scholl was approached by three very official-looking people. One of them whispered something in Mr. Scholl's ear. He looked very **CONCERNED**.

"I wonder what's going on," Huey whispered.

"It doesn't look good," Louie whispered back.

After two more minutes, the official-looking people left. Mr. Scholl scurried over to us.

"What happened?" Louie asked him. "Is everything okay?"

Mr. Scholl hesitated for a second, as if trying to decide whether to tell us. But ultimately, he decided he would.

"No," he said. "Everything is *NOT* entirely okay."

The three of us looked at each other.

"What do you mean?" I asked.

"DR. Z ESCAPED," he told us. "Somehow he invented a contraption that allowed him to melt the steel bars of his jail cell and turn them into yellow gelatin."

We all groaned in shock.

Mr. Scholl's phone buzzed. He glanced at it quickly, then looked back at us. "I must leave you now. Enjoy your time in France, keep in touch, and please come visit us again." We shook hands, and he left.

"Should we be **WORRIED?**" said Louie, who made a habit of being worried.

"Perhaps," I said.

"Why?" Huey said. "We're leaving and he doesn't know where we are going next."

Well, we had our answer when we boarded the plane. In each of our seats was a **SMALL PACKAGE**.

Huey opened his: it was a toy snake.

Louie opened his: it was a globe, with a small crack in it.

Then I opened mine.

It was a miniature version of the Eiffel Tower with a small flag on top with a message.

Three words:

SEE YOU SOON!
SEE YOU SOON!

ABOUT THE AUTHOR

Tommy Greenwald's *Game Changer* is on fourteen state lists, was an Amazon Best Book of the Month, a YALSA Top Ten pick, and a Junior Library Guild Premier selection. Greenwald is also the author of the Crimebiters! and Charlie Joe Jackson series, among many other books for children. Day job–wise, Tommy is the cofounder of Spotco Advertising, a theatrical and entertainment advertising agency in New York City, and the lyricist and co-bookwriter (with Andrew Lippa) of *John & Jen*, an off-Broadway musical that has been produced around the country and internationally. To read woefully outdated information about him, visit tommygreenwald.com.

ABOUT THE ILLUSTRATOR

Elisa Ferrari was born in Verona, Italy, in 1988. She is a self-taught artist. After graduating from university, she started working as an art assistant and then as a complete comic artist and illustrator for different magazines and publishing houses. In Italy she served as an artist for publishing houses like Giunti, Ed. San Paolo, and DeAgostini, and in France, at Edition Jungle, Dargaud, and Drakoo. She is currently working on an unannounced project at Éditions Glénat. Ferarri often collaborates with Arancia Studio, an Italian creative media company.